THE BEST LAID PLANS
of Mice and Men...

BILL SANDS

Copyright © 2011 Bill Sands
All rights reserved.

ISBN: 1460922247
ISBN-13: 9781460922248

DISCLAIMER

The story contained within this book is fictional and in no way represents actual characters or events. All of the activities and individuals are figments of the author's ingenuity; any similarity to actual happenings, or to real persons living or dead, is purely coincidental.

OTHER TITLES BY BILL SANDS

Big Sky and Beyond
Short Story Collection

What Awaits the Dawn
Short Story Collection

Donavan Creek
Modern Western, Novel

I Will Not Die
Short Story Collection

In the Wake of Two Queens
Novel

Off Soundings
Short Story Collection

They Who Dared
Short Story Collection

Alone / Together
Science Fiction, Novel

Libby's Challenge
Novel

Webster's Bay
Novel

BILL SANDS

Bill Sands lives on the North Olympic Peninsula of Washington State far removed from his birthplace and childhood in Massachusetts. He spent a period of his early adulthood living in Tennessee before moving to Montana. He is a veteran of both the U.S. Navy, and the Army National Guard, logging a combined total of over seventeen years in the two services. He is married with four children and a host of other descendants. He has lived in the contemporary settings of small towns as well as wilderness locations in the Montana wilds. For a period of years, he operated a small cattle ranch in Montana and then followed other family members moving westward to Washington State. Here he was involved in a commercial fishing enterprise captaining his own salmon troller and long-line boat. In his retirement years he has furthered his boating interests spending long summers in remote British Columbia waters enjoying his leisure time with his wife Sudie and faithful dog Edward.

THE BEST LAID PLANS
of Mice and Men...

BY
BILL SANDS

(circ. 1970–1991)

Dave Logan rolled into the county seat of Hamilton near noon and parked on the street in front of a small restaurant close to the stockyards. The large number of vehicles, mostly pickups that filled the parking lot to almost overflowing, signified that this was a well-accepted establishment. He ate his meal without haste, choosing to study the clientele rather than hurry. Farming, ranching, and logging were the dominant trades represented here. Several women ate with their companions. There was little makeup visible, not a skirt to be seen, and the only high heels were on the battered cowboy boots worn by many of the men and women present.

In this part of the country, Dave Logan recognized a sense of independence that he had found difficult to locate elsewhere, and he saw some of the results of this freedom here in this room. Other towns during his cross-country journey had been hosting patrons poured from similar molds, most subscribing to the accustomed norms of the social order. Here he suddenly found down-to-earth representatives of hard daily living. Dave saw that he had traveled far enough to leave behind the adherence to fashion trends. He had moved far enough that he was escaping the mainstream of society. Moving farther west would bring him closer to the Pacific, and he would fall back into the quagmire of the upper classes. He paid his check and, with almost a feeling of reluctance, left the warm, friendly atmosphere behind.

Logan was looking for ranch work, but schools had let out the previous week, releasing a flood of eager workers that had quickly filled the few open positions. He bought a newspaper and in the shade of the building front read the classified ads. He stuffed the paper into a trash container beside the restaurant's door and continued his quest. It was beginning to seem quite hopeless, to say the least.

It was nearly 3:00 when he stepped into the K. & C. Feed Mill. Dust hung in the air and clung to everything along with the fragrant odors of many types of grains. He could detect the smell of molasses intermingled with the others. The constant hum and rumble of machinery surrounded the building and caused the floor beneath his feet to vibrate continually. Several people were busy at the counter, and Dave toured the small salesroom while waiting for an opportunity to talk with the clerk.

He noticed a bulletin board on one wall, moved closer for a better view, and found it filled with ranchers' advertisements. Many of the listings were handwritten and were for the sale of used equipment, while others offered livestock and other commodities for sale. His eye paused on a page torn from a small notepad; and he read the hastily printed message.

>HELP WANTED:
>IN EXCHANGE FOR BOARD AND ROOM
>INQUIRE AT
>MARTIN RANCH, WEST FORK ROAD.

A glimmer of hope flashed across Dave Logan's mind. The clerk gave him all the necessary instructions for finding the Martin ranch, and several minutes later Dave left Hamilton and headed south. Some twenty miles down the road, he passed through the small town of Darby, almost before he knew it was there, and checked one waypoint off his mental list of directions. The valley was becoming narrower with mountains beginning to close in on both sides of the highway. The low Sapphire

Mountains to the east, and the towering Bitterroots to the west, met many miles to the south at the Idaho state line. This juncture provided a starting place for the main course of the Bitterroot River.

Logan checked point two off his imaginary list when he reached the fork in the river and turned westward along the smaller of its two tributaries. He was at last traveling up the West Fork Road, and Dave was watching his speedometer closely now. The clerk at the feed mill had given him the approximate mileage, and Dave found that he had covered nearly that distance already. He began slowing at each side road and scanning the mailboxes. So far, each stop had been a false alarm, but this small group was different; one sign above the pair of mailboxes read

THE MARTINS (=M), 4 MILES

Dave turned off the paved highway onto a well-maintained dirt road. Ahead he could see rolling grasslands stretching northward along a broad, steep-sided canyon. Heavily timbered slopes provided a backdrop to the open hay fields. About four miles from the highway, he passed a small ranch. The unpretentious house rested on a slight rise on the left side of the road while the barns, corrals, and other structures were on the right. Dave saw a brightly painted milk-can decorated with daisies fastened atop a fence post. The name on the can was simply,

EDWARDS

He continued straight ahead along the road. A few yards beyond the Edwards' driveway, he rattled across a steel cattle guard. A small sign announced that this was

PRIVATE PROPERTY, THE (=M),
LIVESTOCK AT LARGE

Dave found a scattered line of tall pines bordering both sides of the road, and he drove slowly, studying the terrain. To his right the land rose sharply, the area between the trees choked with heavy underbrush. To his left he could see young stands of hay beyond the screening trees. All was lush and green, and the fences along the road, and those separating the fields, appeared in good condition.

As he climbed higher, things changed gradually. Now, to Dave's left, the slope slanted gently downward into a depression thickly blanketed by a bright green tangle of deciduous trees. "I'll bet there's a creek down there," he thought aloud. At one point, he could see where the invisible stream had cut into the side of a low ridge leaving a steep cliff stretching upward to the overhanging pines above.

When he crested a hill, Logan suddenly saw the ranch headquarters; he stopped in the road for a moment to look over the spread. The small group of buildings rested atop a slight rise on the east side of the valley surrounded by meadows like those on either side of the road. Up-canyon from the ranch, the fields were all sprinkler irrigated; he could see the slowly rotating, pulsing streams of water as they flashed in the late afternoon sun. Dave counted six long lines of sprinklers distributing needed water to the coming crop of hay.

The imposing barn and numerous outbuildings, painted traditional barn red, caused the small one-story white house to stand out boldly from the rest of the structures. From here at least, everything appeared to be in good repair. A solitary milk cow grazed in a small pasture next to the barn. Except for this lone creature, Dave saw no sign of livestock. A few ancient pines were scattered around the house dwarfing the many fruit trees that clustered around the property and along the fence line just above the road. He slipped his car into gear again and drove slowly toward his destination.

Soon the road narrowed, becoming a large circular drive around several of the smaller buildings. A strutting rooster caused him to slow, and a pair of geese screamed a challenge at him when he entered their domain. They fluttered noisily out of his way as he passed. A monstrous animal, that Dave realized was a dog, rose from the ground beside the steps leading to the front door of the house. The animal loped to the driver's side of Dave's car and trotted silently by his side until he parked his car near a battered Volkswagen Bug and a late-model four-wheel-drive pickup. Dave shut off his motor. The huge dog dropped to his haunches and quietly stared at the visitor. The animal's yellow eyes were level with Dave's as the man sat looking around the silent yard. Just north of the house was a large freshly planted garden. Although nearly devoid of vegetation, its well-spaced rows were quite obvious. Between the garden and the barn stretched a long driveway ending at the barred gate of the horse corral. Two horses browsed lazily beside a feeder filled with hay.

"Easy now, big boy," Dave muttered. He very cautiously began to ease his door open. The dog moved back slightly and paced Logan as he walked toward the house. Passing the big pickup, Dave noted that its windows were down, a Winchester carbine hung in a rifle rack across the rear window, and the truck's keys were in the ignition. Dave shook his head and thought aloud, "Trusting souls."

A large gray tomcat crept out of Dave's way when he stepped onto the small porch. At some time in the distant past, the animal had lost all of its tail except for perhaps two inches. The paneled inside door of the house stood open, the house secured by only an unlatched screen door, and this stood ajar. The huge dog assumed a menacing position between Dave and the screen door, dropped to his haunches, and sat silently, his eyes focused intently on Dave's face. In the gloom beyond the open door, Dave saw that the entrance led to the kitchen of the house, not the parlor or living room that would have been the norm in the rest of the country. Dave knocked cautiously at the door twice and, both times, he heard only stillness from within. The rooster crowed mockingly at him from the yard, and the geese honked in harmony as if in reply.

"Oh shut up," Dave muttered.

He turned and moved toward the barn glancing at the machinery in the large equipment sheds as he passed. He saw two tractors. One was a high-wheeled International the other a smaller Ford. An older model Jeep Universal was parked in a small shed next to the barn. The dog walked slowly at his side.

Logan was perhaps fifty feet from the barn when a door banged and a little girl came into view walking toward him carrying an old bucket.

"Hi!" she called. The child struggled with her load, tried to wave, and only partially succeeded. She lugged the battered container with difficulty and transferred it back and forth several times to her other hand. To her it was quite heavy.

"Hi yourself," Logan replied with a smile.

The dog swung quickly aside placing himself between Dave and the little girl. Everyone stopped and the dog let out a very low rumble of warning from deep in his massive chest.

"Down, Wolf," the child snapped.

The dog glanced back at her quickly, the growl faded, and he dropped to a sitting position between them.

The little girl looked to be three or four years old, and her long blond hair hung down her back in a shiny mass of confusion. The child wore blue jeans, with different colored patches in the knees, and a sweatshirt with the arms cut off jaggedly just above her elbows. Dave could see one bare toe trying to poke through the frayed top of a muddy tennis shoe. Her clothes were grimy, but her face was clean, her hair well groomed. Dave frowned. The child's greeting had been happy and friendly, but Dave detected something nearly hidden by her outwardly cheerful disposition; the child seemed almost sad. It was just a hunch, a shadow in the child's eyes that he couldn't put his finger on. Behind the little girl's brief smile, Dave sensed an undercurrent of melancholy.

"Here, let me carry that for you," Dave offered.

The child twisted away slightly, protecting her bucket from his extended hand, and the dog's voice rumbled again. "Down, Wolf!" she snapped. "You behave, now! I can carry it myself," she replied.

"Is he really a wolf?" Dave asked.

"Daddy says he's half."

Dave followed her around the corner of the barn to the pigpen. Two small hogs came to life on seeing her and squealing with anticipation ran excitedly back and forth along the fence.

The child hoisted the heavy bucket to the low railing with both hands, balanced it carefully, and poured it into the trough. The squeals changed to grunts of delight as the pair snorted and groveled their way into the feed.

The girl threw the bucket aside with a clatter, opened a water spigot to added water to the hogs' watering trough, and pointed out the two animals to her visitor. "That's Oink, and the black one's Charlie," she stated as she gave each pig a proper introduction.

"And who are you?" Dave asked.

"Me? I'm Debby! What's your name?"

"Dave, Dave Logan. I'm looking for your dad. Is he around?"

"Mama's out back changing some sprinklers. She'll be back in a little while."

"Where's your dad?"

She twisted the water valve closed. "My daddy's dead."

The thin layer of mock cheerfulness that Dave had first detected was abruptly stripped away, allowing deeper emotions to momentarily surge to the surface. Before Dave could reply, a somber grin returned slowly to her face; she deftly changed the subject. "You want to see my horse?" she asked.

"Sure, let's go see your horse," Dave replied, thankful that the difficult subject had so suddenly been changed.

Debby led the way around the barn to the large corral where Dave again saw two horses standing by a feeder munching hay. The ever-watchful Wolf alertly followed them. The horses raised their heads briefly when the two people stopped beside the wide gate. Debby scrambled like a monkey to the top rail of the shoulder-high enclosure, while Dave leaned against the rails below her. "That's Sam, the black one, he's mine." Debby clapped her hands to get the horse's attention.

"You ride him?" the man asked.

"Oh yes...Come here, Sam, come here," she called, clapping again.

The old black raised his head, glanced toward them, pressed his ears flat against his skull, and with almost a frown resumed eating.

The child explained her mount's reluctance. "He's too hungry right now, but he'll come after he eats."

"Your mother be back pretty soon?" Dave asked.

Debby gestured toward the field on the other side of the open garden area. "She's almost done now," the girl replied.

Dave looked to where the little girl pointed and saw a distant figure carrying a long piece of aluminum irrigation pipe down the slope. The woman paused while she made the connection and then quickly dropped the section in place. Dave could see tiny streams of water spurting feebly from the sprinkler heads along the line she was resetting. She walked back up the slope, picked up another piece, and carried it down to the line. The woman dropped this final section into position and then turned quickly and dashed away from the line. The reason for her burst of speed became apparent a second later when the line of sprinklers burst into full operation.

The woman walked back, parallel to the line, twice darting into the spray to unstop a plugged sprinkler tip. When the obstruction was removed, the head resumed its full operation, and she moved quickly away before the rotating stream could find her.

At the head of the line, she gave a large valve an extra twist or two and then turned to a grazing horse some yards away. She swung into the saddle and at a slow walk headed toward the corral.

"Here she comes now," the child stated.

"Is she all done for the day?"

"We've got to milk the cow. Then we're done."

Dave took interest in the way Debby used the word "we."

As an afterthought the little girl added, "I've got to get my eggs too."

When the rider neared the corral, Logan could see that she wore Levis and knee-high rubber boots. The sleeves of the woman's light chambray shirt were soaked from her elbows down, and an old wide-brimmed hat was cocked over her eyes shading them from the glare of the late afternoon sun. From the condition of the battered headgear Dave guessed that it was probably a family heirloom, undoubtedly handed down through several generations.

The gap between the big equipment gate and the corner of the barn contained a small portal just big enough for a man, and the little girl climbed down and started toward this smaller opening. "I've got to open the gate for Mama."

"I'll get it for you," Dave offered. He moved into the enclosure and crossed to the far side just as the woman approached. Dave opened the gate enough for her to pass.

She thumbed her hat onto the back of her head, glanced quizzically at the stranger, and neck-reined her mount into the corral. "Evening," she greeted.

"Nice one, isn't it," Dave remarked. He swung the bars closed and dropped the latch into place.

The woman wheeled her horse about and backed the animal several paces. "I'll be with you as soon as I turn this guy loose." She swung the big gelding quickly across the corral.

Dave walked back toward the child waiting by the other gate with her dog. The woman dismounted by the barn and began pulling the gear from her horse. The doorway to the small tack room had a heavy bar across its opening to keep the horses out. She ducked under this obstacle and lugged the heavy saddle into the room. A moment later she returned, stripped the bridle from her horse's head, gave him a slap, and chased him out into the open corral.

The horse bucked, his head tucked low against his chest, his hind legs kicking at the wind. He snorted and pawed, threw himself down, and with four legs flailing in the air ground dirt deep into his back. After this, he rose, shook out a cloud of dust, and trotted to a small stream of water running along the far side of the corral.

The woman joined Dave and her daughter by the gate. "Crazy damned animal," she muttered.

Debby was again perched high on the top rail of the gate, and the woman reached up toward her with outstretched arms. The child closed her eyes and just toppled forward, and her mother caught her as she fell. It was obvious that they often played this game. Dave Logan scanned the woman carefully while she playfully ruffled her daughter's hair. Her attractiveness threw him off guard momentarily, and deep within a warning sounded that he quickly shoved aside. The woman dropped Debby to the ground, pulled off her bedraggled hat, and fanned herself briefly. She hung the hat on a fence post, dried her face and neck with an old bandanna, and returned this to the hip pocket of her grimy jeans.

"Mama, this is Dave," the girl began. "He wanted to see Daddy...I told him you'd be back soon."

"Well, Mr. Dave, welcome to the Double Bar M. I'm Peg Martin. My husband died awhile back so I guess you'll have to do business with me. I see you've met Wolf already... God, it's hot today, isn't it."

The woman extended her hand to him. When Dave took her offered palm, he noticed three things: the missing end of her index finger, the callused roughness of her hand, and the strength of her grip.

"Yes, it's pretty warm. Last name's Logan, Dave Logan. Debby told me about her dad. I'm sorry."

"You been waiting long?" she asked ignoring Dave's remark about her husband.

"No! Only a few minutes," he replied.

Peg Martin's clothes were dirty, faded, and worn; her jeans were cinched about her waist by a hand-tooled leather belt. She wore her belt buckle off center, forward of her left hipbone, for comfort. The ornate stainless steel buckle was done in relief showing the image of a riderless bucking horse. The irrigating chores she had just completed had gotten the front of her jeans quite damp, almost wet. He guessed that she was in her late thirties; but her dark complexion, slight sunburn, and a questioning frown of uncertainty, was masking her age well. She was a tall woman and carried her weight easily on a large frame. It took only a second for Dave to see that she was quite well built, and he broke off his scrutiny quickly when he realized that he was staring.

"I saw your *help wanted* notice in Hamilton today," he began.

The woman interrupted him, "Let's get out of the sun."

They left the corral through the narrow gate and started down the long drive toward the house. Peg placed her old hat on Debby's head while they walked along. The little girl clung playfully to her mother's thigh for a moment causing the woman to limp heavily under the burden. After several yards, the woman emphatically pushed her away. They stopped beside the garden fence where the lofty barn gave them some shade.

Peg took back her hat, hung it on a post, and ran work-worn fingers through her short, dark, wavy hair. Dave noted the tiny silver studs in her ear lobes standing out brightly against her dark skin. This was the only open concession to femininity that he could detect.

Peg Martin looked steadily at Logan for long moments, and her deep blue eyes searched him intently while she shook her head slowly side to side. "I'd hoped for someone younger." The woman made this comment while Debby again swung on her leg. "Excuse me just a minute," she added apologetically. Bending down to her daughter she said, "OK, Spider, let go now! Enough's enough! How about finishing your chores."

"I'll get my eggs later," the girl replied.

"Nope! You go get them now!"

"Can't Mr. Logan help me?" Debby asked.

The woman turned the child in the direction of the chicken house and gave her a gentle shove. "No he can't! Git! Now!"

"Oh well, I guess it's man's talk." The child darted off across the yard. She ran only a few feet, stopped, and looked around. "I'll be right back!" she called.

The woman pointed with the stub of her finger toward the barn. "Get going!" she ordered.

As the child turned to go, she called again, "I know; I won't break any." Debby dashed off as fast as she could run, vanishing around the corner of the barn in seconds.

Peg chuckled and shook her head in mock disbelief. "Well now, where was I? Oh, like I said, I was hoping for someone younger, some high school kid who would simply like to get out of town for the summer, or something like that; regardless, you're the first prospect I've had, and it's been over a week now."

Dave made an open admission. "I've got a strong back but no experience, Mrs. Martin."

Peg frowned, and then she went on, seeming to ignore his statement. "You know from my notice that it's only room and board, no wages? Times are really hard since…"

Dave interrupted her, "Yes, I know. That's OK."

"How the hell do you plan to make out with no wages?" she inquired.

"I'm retired Air Force. I finished my time last month, and I'll have a pension coming in regularly, so today money is no real object."

"If money isn't the object, what is? Grown men don't just offer to work for nothing. You could take a nice vacation if you wanted, so why stop off here and work for nothing?" Before Dave could reply, she had another thought. "You hiding from somebody?" The woman asked her questions frankly, and Dave could tell that she was openly puzzled and concerned.

"No! I'm not hiding, or running. I've been thinking about buying a small ranch and working it now that I'm retired. I've invested and saved for a long time, and now that I'm free, I'm about ready to make my move. Right now, I'm trying to find work on a ranch for a full year. It would be a learning experience for me, on-the-job training, and would give me a better idea of whether I'd like ranching or not. Maybe I'm not cut out for this way of life, who knows."

Peg's eyebrows rose slightly. "Oh! You want to stay a full year?"

"Yes, if possible. The experience would be worth a million bucks to me if I did buy a place of my own."

"What about your family?" she questioned.

"I was divorced years ago. No kids and no strings attached."

"Oh." Peg nodded thoughtfully while she retrieved her hat from the post, and then she began walking slowly along the fence. She dragged her left hand along the top rail of the shoulder-high fence in almost a caressing manner while her eyes studied the dirt driveway beneath her feet.

Dave Logan matched her stride, and they were nearly to the corner of the garden before she stopped and spoke again.

Peg Martin turned an inquisitive, almost pretty face toward him. "You don't know anything about ranching, or any of this?" She made a wide sweeping gesture with her arm.

"Almost nothing," he admitted. "But I worked on a dairy farm one summer when I was a kid."

"You'd take room and board like I offered, no wages?"

"That's right!"

They passed the corner of the equipment shed walking slowly and silently toward the house. The pair of white geese that he had seen when he arrived darted toward them, necks outstretched, threatening. Peg took her battered hat and threw it like a Frisbee at the lead goose. The hisses changed to raucous honking while they strutted away in elegant retreat. Wolf bounded toward the two geese, stopping to retrieve Peg's hat. He trotted back with the headgear crushed tightly in his massive jaws. Peg grabbed her hat without breaking stride and slapped the dirt from it before returning it to her head.

"Thank you, Wolf," she muttered ruffling the dog's coat.

"I got nine," yelled a small voice behind them. Debby moved briskly across the yard carrying a small plastic bucket that obviously contained her treasury of eggs.

"You shut the door tight?" her mother asked.

Debby smiled. "Sure, don't I always?"

The woman corrected her daughter. "No! Not always! Go wash them off, Spider, and put them in the fridge. We'll be there in just a minute."

"OK," she answered and moved off toward the house.

"She's quite a girl, isn't she," Dave stated.

Peg agreed. "Yes! She's hard to keep up with." The woman frowned suddenly. "She sure seems awful damned happy all of a sudden."

"How old is she?

"She'll be six in November."

"When did you say her father died?" Dave watched carefully for the woman's reaction to his probing question.

"I didn't, but Lou died in March. Just about three months ago." Peg showed no outward emotion to the question or to its obviously difficult answer.

"It must be hard running the place alone."

"It's damned hard, but I've managed so far. What's more, I'm not alone. The big jobs like the roundup and branding, the neighbors pitch in and help. Out here, we all help each other. Always have. Furthermore, I've got Spider. She's only five, but you'd be surprised how much help she is. But wait a minute, we've gotten way off the subject. We were talking about you. You want the job on my terms?"

"Yes, Ma'am!"

Peg Martin looked him up and down carefully, her frown of uncertainty changing to just a trace of a smile. She took a deep breath of air and exhaled it slowly while she made her final decision. "OK, Mr. David Logan, ex-Air Force. As of now, you're a cowboy; at least I'll try turning you into one. Any questions?"

"Just one right now. Where are all your cattle?"

The woman laughed and waved her arm toward the mountains north of the ranch. "Back in the foothills right now. I've got a Forest Service grazing permit. Works out well. We'll bring them in here just for the winter. Any more questions?"

"A million, Mrs. Martin, but they can wait. Thanks for the chance."

"Let's start out with first names, all right? We can't work together with all this formality and all these Mr. and Mrs. flying back and forth."

"Fine by me," he replied.

* * *

They entered the house, and Wolf curled up against the bottom step of the porch. Dave found himself in a cluttered kitchen. A small step stool stood before the sink where water still ran, and Debby was placing her freshly washed eggs into the refrigerator. Peg hung her hat on a hook beside the screen door and crossed to the sink where she turned off the faucet. She pulled off her irrigation boots, and kicked them over beside the back door. She shuffled across the kitchen wearing only the heavy boot socks on her feet. Peg's right sock had slipped partway down the calf of her leg allowing the loose foot of her sock to flop and flap ahead of her as she walked, creating a comical picture, to say the least.

"I'll bet you haven't eaten, have you?" she inquired, bending down and tugging the loose sock back into place.

Dave glanced around at the untidy kitchen. "No! Have you?"

"We eat early, about four during the summer. Then I change the lines and we finish up the chores. It's usually a little cooler working that way."

"No problem at all, Peg. Just a cup of coffee will tide me over till morning. I had a big lunch."

"You're on the payroll, and the payroll's room and board. The least I can do is fix you something. If you like leftovers, it won't take me a minute, if you don't like leftovers, you're out of luck."

"Leftovers will be fine," he replied.

"Are you going to work here?" the child asked as she completed her job.

"I sure am, Debby."

"Whoopee! Now you can feed the pigs and collect the eggs for me."

Peg cut in quickly. "No way, young lady! He'll have his own work to do, same as you."

"You'd be a better egg collector anyway, Debby," Dave added. "Besides, I'm scared of chickens." Dave caught Peg's eye and winked.

"Oh, yes, I guess so. You'd probably break them anyway." After a short pause Debby added, "You can call me Spider, Mr. Logan."

"OK! But only if you call me Dave."

"Hold on," Peg interrupted swinging quickly from the counter to face them. "First names are fine, but let's not have any nicknames tossed around. Debra, you go to the bathroom and get washed up, right now!"

The snap in the woman's voice surprised him. A sore spot must have been touched. Obviously, the woman's tone had signaled something to the child as well, for Debby had turned and left the room quickly, without comment.

Peg glanced after her daughter, looked back at Dave, lowered her voice to almost a whisper, and explained. "Dave, Spider is a pretty special nickname that her dad gave her. I have no idea where Lou picked up that nickname. I'd really appreciate it if you wouldn't use it. I think you can understand why."

"Sure, I'll just call her Debby."

"Thanks! I've gotten into the habit of calling her Spider most times myself," Peg whispered. In her normal voice she continued, "Go in the living room and make yourself at home. I'll have this heated up in just a little."

Dave walked through the doorway to the living room, a cozy and obviously well-lived-in area of the small house. In the corner, to the left of the kitchen doorway, stood a modern wood-burning heater and, in the opposite corner, a small television. A couch and several chairs provided ample seating and added to the comfortable atmosphere of the room. The coffee table and two end tables were heaped with a collection of magazines and farm and ranch publications. From the depth of the collection, it became obvious that some items must have been at least six months old. Topping the stacks of periodicals were several pieces of clothing, mostly the child's, with more scattered about the room at random. It was obvious that Peg Martin devoted herself to the outside business of running the ranch and had little time or energy for the housekeeping chores that occupied most women. After moving several newspapers, a child's sweater, and a stray red tennis shoe, Dave dropped into an easy chair where he could watch the woman working in the kitchen. Peg paused in her cooking to hand him a cup of coffee.

Debby suddenly darted into the room, dug through the litter on the large coffee table, and handed him one of her favorite books. "Read me a story," she suggested, crawling up on the arm of his chair.

Dave took the book and began to read. The little girl leaned back with one arm around his shoulders where she could see the pictures better. Debby smelled like fresh soap as she snuggled against him listening to the story about a little girl and her pony.

While he read, he glanced now and then at the child's mother as she prepared his meal. Although busy in the kitchen, Peg had found time to wash up and brush her hair. The sleeves of her shirt had dried, and Dave Logan realized that his employer was looking better all the time.

Occasionally Peg would lean back comfortably against the counter with her arms folded across her chest. When first glancing her way, Dave would detect a slight frown etched into the dark surface of her face. When their eyes met, Peg would flash a thin smile, and then would quickly turn back to tend to the coming meal. Dave finished his coffee, and Debby's book, just as Peg announced that his supper was ready. It was obvious that she knew the story, for she had awaited her notification until he had said, "The end."

Debby jumped down from the chair and, taking his hand, dragged him into the kitchen. The table still contained an assortment of odds and ends from previous meals, and the counter by the sink was piled with dirty dishes. Everything seemed to be in complete confusion and utterly out of control.

"You can sit here," Debby said. "This was Daddy's seat," and she steered Dave toward a place at the head of the table. "This is my seat right here," the child added.

"Hold on, Spider. Not so quick. You can't give away my place," Peg corrected.

"But, Dave's here now."

"Don't argue! Dave, sit across from Debby, if you will."

He took the indicated seat without comment. Peg had heated up a plate of leftover casserole, fresh garden peas from her freezer, warmed-over biscuits, and sliced green peppers. She put the meal in front of him and rummaged through a drawer beside the sink to find his silverware. Peg deposited these items in a pile beside his plate. While Dave began to eat, she served three large slices of apple pie, added strips of cheese to the top, and joined them at the table.

Peg started eating her pie right away, but Debby ignored the piece before her. She sat with her elbows on the wood surface, her head cradled in her hands watching the man eat. Dave hadn't realized how hungry he really was until he began.

Debby whispered to her mother from behind a shielding hand. "He's real hungry, Mama. I think he likes it." She didn't take her eyes off their new hired man for even an instant as she spoke.

"Deborah," her mother cautioned.

Dave glanced up from his meal. "That's OK! She's right," he admitted. "This is good, Peg, really hits the spot."

"It's nice to know you don't mind leftovers."

"If this is leftover, I'll bet the original meals are super."

"Mama's a real good cook," Debby added.

"Eat your pie," Peg suggested.

"I'm waiting for Dave."

He finished his meal shortly, slid the dinner plate aside, and drew the apple pie toward him. "OK, Debby, now let's eat our pie," he prompted.

The child grinned broadly at him, picked up her fork, and began to eat. Peg had finished her piece and turned to the stove to fill Dave's cup. She set the brimming mug beside his plate and began washing the pile of dishes. Dave and Debby finished their pie, gathered the dirty dishes from the table, and carried them to the counter.

"Thanks," Peg said. "Debby, did you feed Wolf?"

"Not yet."

"Better get with it."

"Want me to dry those dishes, Peg?" Dave asked.

"Lord no! We never do. I just stack them in the drainer and they dry themselves. You can pour me a cup of coffee, if you will. My cup's somewhere over there." Peg canted her head in the direction of the far counter. "It's the one with the railroad locomotive on it." She paused for a moment and tugged her loose sock back into place again.

Dave poured and set the cup within her reach. While she worked, he leaned back against the counter and they chatted about the ranch. She began a very lengthy list of the various chores that had to be done, many of them on a daily, or twice-daily basis. Then there were the seasonal happenings. Many of these were monumental. They usually turned out to be almost community ventures, with each rancher pitching in with his neighbor, pooling their resources to finish the job.

Following her husband's death, Peg must have been faced with what seemed like an impossible task. The scope of her undertaking appeared awesome. Dave wondered how she had planned to do the job if he or someone else hadn't come along to accept her "room and board" proposition. He looked at the tall, attractive woman beside him for a long moment and figured that she would have persevered and would have found some way regardless of the odds.

Peg finished the stack of dishes, wiped the counters and table clean, dried her hands on the back of her jeans, and heaved a long sigh of relief. The kitchen was ready for the onslaught that would begin the following day.

She turned to Dave. "The bathroom's in there," and she nodded to the door off the side of the kitchen. "You'll have everything you need in the bunkhouse, even hot water, except for a tub. When you want to take a bath just give me a little warning. The house is never locked so come and go as you please. One thing though, we go to bed pretty early, nine or nine thirty usually. I'd like you to clear out at the same time, OK?"

"Sure thing," Dave replied.

"There's only one station on the TV and the reception's not all that great. Help yourself. The phones in the office but go easy on long distance calls."

"Don't need to make any."

"Good. I'll show you the bunkhouse as soon as I get some covers. I'll just be a minute."

Peg turned through a door behind the kitchen and entered her bedroom. She returned a few minutes later carrying a couple of blankets and other pieces of bedding. Peg placed the bedding on the seat of a kitchen chair and stopped beside the back door. Balancing carefully she pulled her flopping socks up tight and one by one wiggled her feet into battered riding boots. Peg gathered up the bedding and straightened up. Dave was surprised at how tall she suddenly appeared. Her high-heeled riding boots had made a significant difference.

When they passed the living room, Debby yelled, "Wait for me!"

"Shut off that TV," her mother reminded.

The little girl skidded to a halt in the kitchen and dashed back to switch off the set. It was turning cool already, and the remaining sliver of sun would be gone behind the distant peaks in less than a minute. Debby raced across the yard, gathered the big gray tomcat in her arms, and lugged him back toward Dave and her mother.

"This is George," she announced.

"Hi, George," Dave replied, reaching down to pat the cat's head.

The beast let out almost a growl and, twisting in the child's arms, struck at Dave's hand. Dave drew back just in time. Debby tried to hold the cat, but lost her battle and dropped the squirming animal to the ground.

"He isn't very friendly to strangers," Debby confessed. "But don't worry, Dave; he'll learn to like you."

The child's mother was just entering the small building between the house and the barn. Both ends of the structure were open carports, presently unoccupied, and between these was the small bunkhouse. It was nothing more than an average-sized room and contained a bed, chest of drawers, small couch, table, and two straight chairs. With all the furnishings, it was crowded; but it appeared to be comfortable. On one side of the room was a closet and adjoining it a small bathroom, complete, as Peg had said, except for a tub.

Peg Martin deposited the armload of bedding on the unmade bed. "This building's well insulated. It used to be for fruit storage or canned goods so it stays pretty comfortable year round. That electric heater has a thermostat. If you get cold, just turn it on and set it where you want it. Right now, we'll air everything out a little." Peg turned and opened the lone window in the bunkhouse's east wall.

"OK! This looks like it will do just fine."

"Good. You get settled in. I've got to go milk the cow."

"Need any help?" Dave asked.

"No. Not tonight, just get settled. Come on, Spider."

"I want to help Dave, Mama."

"You have to get Elsie for me, remember? You can come back afterward, come on now!"

The child ducked past her mother and then stopped at the open doorway. "I'll be back in just a minute, Dave."

"Slow down, Debby. You'll run out of gas," he replied.

She made Dave a promise, "No, I won't!" and headed full tilt for the corner of the barn. Peg shook her head in disbelief and followed her daughter without comment.

Dave stood in the doorway for a long minute and watched Peg Martin while she walked toward the barn. In her battered riding boots, she seemed taller; without a hat, her hair caught the last rays of the sun reflecting back a deep auburn hue that he hadn't realized before was there. Dave could think of only one adequately descriptive word while he watched her move away. He nodded in quiet approval and muttered, "Nice."

The sun had dropped behind the peaks and darkness was descending quickly. He unlocked the trunk of his car and began unloading his few possessions.

Debby raced down the drive from the barn. "Wait a minute. I'm coming!" she called.

"Shouldn't you be helping your mother?" Dave asked when Debby pulled up beside him.

"Oh, no! I'm done! All I had to do was open the gate, chase Elsie into the stall, and give her her grain. Mama does the rest." The child was panting slightly from her fast round trip to the barn.

Dave handed her a small traveling bag. "OK, Debby. Here, you can take this in for me."

He grabbed an armload of luggage and followed the child into the bunkhouse where Debby helped him unpack. A few minutes later, he slid his two empty suitcases under the bed and moved the pile of bedding from the mattress to the seat of a chair. Without comment, Debby sprang around to the other side of the bed and helped him with the bottom sheet. It was obvious that she had performed this task before; and in no time, they had made the bed.

Logan turned from the bed and confronted Peg Martin standing in the open doorway. She leaned comfortably against the doorjamb watching them work. Peg's arms were folded gracefully, her weight resting on one leg while the other was hooked casually behind.

"Well, you two work fast," she remarked, catching his eye. "Is there anything else you need, Dave?"

"I don't think so."

"Well, we'd better get to bed. You know it's almost ten?"

"That late?" he asked glancing at his watch.

"It stays light pretty late out here," she explained. "Come on, Spider. Tell Dave good night."

"Can't I stay with Dave a little longer?" the child asked.

"No, you can't! Get going and crawl into bed. I'll be in to kiss you in a minute." Peg turned the child gently and eased her out the door.

Debby twisted away from her mother's hand and reached up for Dave Logan's arms. He stooped down and accepted the child's hug. Dave held her close for a brief moment, turned her toward the door, and gave her a push. "Go to bed, Debby. I'll see you in the morning."

"Good night, Dave," she called. Before the sound of her voice faded, she was already in full flight toward the house.

"Have you got an alarm clock?" Peg inquired.

"Yes."

"Breakfast will be at six. We start work about seven. I'll see you then."

"I'll be ready," he promised.

"Night, Dave."

"Good night, Peg, and thanks."

She left without further comment waving a tired hand to him in parting. Dave retrieved the few remaining items from his car and paused before entering the doorway. It was completely dark by this time, and the air had turned almost cold. The front of the small house was dark but, in the back, he could see the glimmer of light from one of the bedroom windows.

The "Big Sky of Montana" stretched above him adorned by a trillion stars that were so close that he felt he could touch them. In the distance, Dave could hear the rhythmic click, click, click of numerous sprinkler heads as they continued their work throughout the night. Closer at hand a chicken squawked, and fluttered for a moment as it apparently fell from the crowded roost.

Dave closed his door against the chill and dug his old hiking boots from the bottom of the closet. His heavy Levi jacket would probably feel good in the morning, and he hung it on a hook beside the door. Logan wound his clock and set his alarm, turned off the light, and dropped onto the bed. Dave grinned while thinking of Debby, but the grin faded as he remembered a fleeting glimpse into her somber inner personality. He realized how difficult it must have been for the child to loose her father at such a young age.

He pictured Debby's mother, strong, capable, and attractive. He could only imagine the deep hurt, the sudden loneliness that she had felt and endured following the death of her husband. He was asleep in minutes, surrounded by only the ticking of his alarm and the faint rattling sounds of the sprinkler heads in the field.

* * *

Dave awoke with a start the following morning. The blackness of night still gripped the room, and a chill hovered around him while he rested warm and snug beneath his blankets. The sound that had stirred him initially cut through the stillness again as a rooster crowed his raucous challenge to the coming day. Dave rose to one elbow and glanced across the room at his alarm. The luminous hands showed five fifteen. He flipped back the covers and shut off the clock before it had a chance to compete with the rooster, again crowing somewhere nearby.

Dave pulled back the curtain and peered out. It was still dark, but the approaching day had begun to silhouette the mountains along the eastern horizon. Light streamed from the front windows of the house, and he detected smoke rising from the chimney. He closed the bunkroom window and turned back to the room. It was quite cold, and Dave snapped on the small electric heater to knock the chill out of the air.

Logan flipped on the light and squinted against its sudden glare. He pulled on his jeans and turned to the sink to get ready for the day. While he shaved, he heard the faint click of a latch and suddenly felt a cold draft across his bare back. He could see the outside door plainly in the mirror as it was slowly pushed open. Debby Martin peeked cautiously into the room while he watched.

The child slipped into the bunkhouse and quietly eased the door closed behind her. She wore a warm quilted coat, a stocking cap, and an impish grin. Her early morning cheerfulness brought a quick smile to Dave's eyes, but he pretended to be unaware of her presence. He continued to shave and from the corner of his eye watched while she tiptoed across the room to the open doorway behind him. Debby stopped by the jamb and with a look of curiosity watched the man before her. He finished shaving and rinsed the shaving cream remnants from his face.

"Boo!" he snapped, turning suddenly and stooping down to face the small child. "What are you doing here?" Debby jumped visibly, a startled look streaking across her face, and she took two quick steps backward in retreat.

"Hi, Debby. What'd I do, scare you?" Dave dropped to one knee to remain face-to-face with the child.

A scowl of irritation played across Debby's face, and she shook her head at him, making her stocking cap flap comically. "You shouldn't scare people early in the morning," she responded.

"Sorry about that, but you know, little girls should knock on a door before they come barging in."

"I'm sorry. I'll knock next time."

"I'm sorry I scared you. Still friends?" he asked offering her his hand.

The child ignored his outstretched hand and threw her arms around his neck in a meaningful hug. "You're my friend," she replied.

Dave squeezed her briefly in return and slipped into his shirt. Sitting down on the unmade bed, he began pulling on his boots. "Breakfast ready?" he asked.

Debby turned quickly toward the door. "Oh, I almost forgot," she began. "Mama sent me after a jug of milk," and she reached for the knob.

"Where's the milk?"

"Out in the cooler in the milk room. I'll be right back," she promised and dashed out the door.

Dave Logan made up his bed for the day, slipped into his jacket and baseball cap, and stepped out into the yard. On the outside wall of the bunkhouse, he noted a large circular thermometer, its needle sitting plainly on a chilly twenty-eight degrees. He waited for Debby in the predawn shadows, watching his breath drift before him in vaporous swirls. When she arrived he took the gallon jug of milk from her arms, and she immediately thrust her cold hands underneath the bottom of her coat where it was warm. Nearing the porch, Dave could see the child's mother moving about her chores in the kitchen. Everything appeared warm and cheery, and he and the little girl entered the room together.

"I watched Dave shave, Mama," Debby stated.

Peg glanced over her shoulder at them when they entered. She wore the same clothes that she had worn the day before and was tucking the tails of her grimy shirt into her jeans with one hand while turning pancakes with the other.

"Morning, Dave. Has she been bothering you?"

"No! Not at all," he replied. "Where do you want the milk?"

"Just put it over there on the counter," she ordered, pointing with the spatula. "Spider, take your coat off and go brush the rat's nests out of your hair or no breakfast for you." Peg tossed her instructions over her shoulder while she slid steaming pancakes from the grill, onto a plate in the warm oven.

The child pulled off her hat and coat and threw them in the general direction of the living room couch. She raced on at almost a gallop, heading for her bedroom. Dave pulled off his jacket and cap and laid them across the arm of the chair. He noted that a fire was burning in the woodstove and stepped close to soak up its warmth. There was just a hint of wood smoke in the air.

"This is June! Is it always this cold in the morning?" he asked as Peg handed him a cup of coffee through the doorway.

"Not usually, but once in a while. It'll be hell changing pipes this morning, you can bet on that. I've seen a few times that the grass was covered with tiny ice crystals that rattled and cracked under your boots. Not cold enough today for that though."

Dave picked Debby's coat up from the floor and put it on the couch with her cap.

"I'm ready to eat," Debby said as she skipped across the room and wiggled into her chair at the table.

"OK, come on, both of you, it's ready!"

While they ate, Dave glanced through the kitchen windows, glimpsing the first rays of the coming day as they reflected off the distant snowcapped peaks to the west. Country sausage, thick buttermilk pancakes laced with huckleberries, a heaping mound of hash brown potatoes, and whole wheat toast with jelly went down quickly. He was finishing his second cup of coffee when Peg left the table and went into her bedroom. She returned a moment later with a pair of knee-high irrigation boots and dropped them beside his chair.

"Here, your feet look as big as Lou's. Try these on."

Without comment, Dave unlaced his hiking boots and tried on the rubber footwear. The thought of *filling another man's shoes* flashed through his mind. Although these fit perfectly, he knew that he'd never be able to fill them completely.

Peg pulled on her boots and an incredibly dirty Levi jacket, crammed her worn hat onto her head, and reached for the door. Their day had begun.

The sun was just breaking free of the horizon, casting a bright fresh glow the full length of the canyon.

"Get Elsie in, Spider," Peg ordered and turning to Dave, she said, "I milk the cow first, then we'll get started on the lines. You can feed the horses; there's hay in the pickup. Give them a little over a bale. Debby will open the gate for you."

"OK. Where's the keys?" Dave asked, forgetting for the moment that he had seen them in the truck the day before.

"In the rig. I never take them out."

Debby had gone to bring in the cow while her mother and Dave talked, and she was at the corral to open the gate for him when he arrived with the truck and the hay. She stood guard at the open gate while he unloaded the hay and then swung the heavy bars closed behind him when he left. Dave parked the truck beside the house and walked back toward the barn. He glanced around; the child was nowhere to be seen.

It took Logan several minutes to find the milking room in the dim, unfamiliar interior of the barn. A small Guernsey cow standing quietly in a stanchion looked up briefly when he entered and then went back to eating her ration of grain. Peg sat on a milking stool while rich streams of milk rattled into the pail between her knees. Wisps of steam, rising from the bucket in the cold morning air carried the sweet aroma of fresh milk throughout the room. Dave hadn't sensed this fragrance in over twenty years.

"Want me to finish up?" he asked.

"You can try."

He changed places with the woman and with a feeling of uncertainty reached for the task at hand. Much to his surprise, he found that his summer on a dairy farm, so many years ago, hadn't been wasted. Following a moment's hesitation, the streams began to flow rhythmically.

"Well I'll be damned," Peg muttered in surprise.

Dave grinned at her over his shoulder. "I told you I worked on a dairy farm once," he replied.

"Yeah, when you were a kid. I remember."

"Where's Debby?" Dave asked.

"Feeding her pigs, I guess."

"What does she do all day while you're working?"

"Plays around here. She has the swing, a tricycle, and her toys. If I'm going to be gone for too long she goes down to the Edwards' place. Sometimes I take her and sometimes she rides old Sam down and back. When Lou was alive, we never left her alone. Now? Well, it's a different story now. I know there's a danger, but she minds the rules very well. She has her work to do too. She's supposed to feed Wolf, clean up the kitchen table, and sweep the floor, little things like that, but she usually doesn't get a great deal done. I don't push much; she's still pretty young. She never forgets Wolf and always does real well with her outside chores; I honestly can't complain."

Dave had reached the stripping process when George the cat arrived meowing loudly. Peg picked up a dirty bowl and, reaching past Dave's shoulder, extended it low enough to catch the dwindling streams. Dave aimed carefully and filled the cat's dish half full. Peg placed it in the corner for the happy feline.

"Like I said, if I have to be away from the house for too long, I take Debby down to Beth Edwards. You passed their place on the way up here. Sometimes I even let her ride Sam down there on her own. Beth and Glenn take good care of her for me when the need arises. With Wolf here I don't worry about strangers."

They finished the milking, released the cow, and strained, bottled, and stowed the milk in the large cooler. After washing the items they had used, they were ready for the outside chores.

"You a horseman?" she asked.

Dave felt a flutter of uncertainty at her words. "Not yet," he replied.

"We'll use just mine to start with today. I'll break you in on a horse later this morning. It's a little work to saddle up, but it beats walking all that way."

Peg got her gear, then roped and saddled her big gelding, Gus. She explained in detail every step of the process. Peg finished saddling, gathered up her reins, and leading her mount headed for the fields afoot. They moved side by side down the gentle slope along the main irrigation line, and Peg continued to explain things while they walked. They finally reached the lower sprinkler setting, and Peg dropped the reins of her bridle ground-reining her horse and allowing him to graze.

Peg shut off the line, removed the heavy valve assembly, and hooked it back up to the next outlet forty feet down the line. She opened the valve part way. They began unhooking the sections of pipe and moving them down the field. As they worked, a large volume of water flowed from the open end of the pipe flushing out the sand and debris that lay in the line. Peg worked with him, section by section, explaining the process, giving him tips, and showing him how. At last, she dropped the final pipe into place and moved quickly back out of the way. This section had a plug installed in its open end. With no place for the water to go, the line filled quickly, thumped, and jerked one time as it came under pressure and blossomed into full operation. They ducked away from the pulsing jets of water and walked back along the line. Peg handed Dave a small piece of wire from her jacket pocket. He used this wire like a pick when they stopped twice to unclog plugged-up sprinkler tips. Due to Dave's lack of experience, setting the line was a lengthy process, but finally one line was finished.

Peg opened the valve fully, gathered the reins of her mount, and swung aboard. She would start at the top of the far field and work down while Dave would start from here. They would meet somewhere in the middle. She rode off at a gentle lope, leaving him to the chore at hand. They met almost two hours later. Of the five remaining lines, Peg had changed four, and Dave one.

Peg led her horse through a side gate into the ranch house yard. "Let's go get warmed up," she suggested.

Dave didn't argue; he was soaked and his hands were nearly frozen. Peg tied the horse to a fence rail in front of Dave's car and they walked to the door. Dave noticed the redness of her hands when she stretched them out over the warmth of the woodstove and saw that his were a much brighter red. In comparison, it was easy to see who was accustomed to this way of life, and who was not.

Peg threw her jacket aside and a moment later returned from the kitchen with coffee for them both. Dave could see a steady curtain of steam rising from the legs of Peg's jeans as they dried and could feel the heat soaking in across his wet thighs as well. Time and again, he was forced to turn the other side when the damp material against his legs became too hot to bear.

Before too long, they were warm and almost dry. While changing their footwear, Debby entered the house with her eggs. "I got eleven, Mama," she exclaimed.

"Good girl! Wash them off before you put 'em away."

The child turned to the sink while the adults got ready to leave. The moment of silence was suddenly broken by an ominous sound, "*Plop*," followed by the child's quiet exclamation, "Woops."

"How many do you have now?" Peg asked.

"I don't know. I'll count them."

"I think you've got ten now, but you check and see. Clean up the mess when you get done."

A slight touch of exasperation had edged into Peg's voice during the brief exchange, and she had addressed her daughter without once looking toward the sink.

"You're right, Mom, ten. Gee you're so smart."

"Eleven take away one is...?" Peg began.

"I'll get George to clean this up. Cats like egg."

"OK, but then clean up after George...By the way, the answer is ten," Peg replied.

Peg untied her mount from the fence, and the two adults left for the corral leaving Debby to solve her own morning problems.

"Never trust a damned horse, Dave," had been Peg's one curt warning as he began his first riding lesson. She had him saddle Debby's old black two times until she felt he could manage by himself.

Debby arrived with Wolf, after completing her chores, and perched high atop the bars of the corral gate. "Be careful of Sam, Dave. He's real old," she called.

"Better tell Sam to be careful of me," he suggested, and the child let out a hearty laugh in reply.

A half hour of saddle time taught him plenty, and Peg decided that he was ready for a younger, more spirited animal. "OK, now let's try a real horse," she exclaimed.

"What's the matter with, Sam?" Debby asked, hurt slightly by her mother's insinuation.

"He's a good old horse for you, Spider, but that's about all." Peg turned to Dave and explained. "He's so old that he won't run at all. If you work on him hard you can maybe get him to trot a little, but that's about it. For her, he's rock steady and dependable, that's why I keep him."

"How old is he?" Dave asked.

Peg laughed. "Lou used to say that '*he was a week older than God.*' We really have no idea how old he is. He has no papers, and his teeth are so bad that the vets can't even tell."

Peg picked up an old lariat hanging by the tack room doorway. She shook out a loop and flipped it deftly into place on the remaining horse's neck.

"This little mare is called Goldie. She's a darn good horse for working cattle. She'll help you a lot if you just give her the idea."

While Dave saddled the small roan mare, Peg shortened the stirrups on Sam's saddle for her daughter. They were snubbed up short in the very last notch. Debby led her old black to the feed bunk and, using it as a step, managed to reach the stirrup and climb aboard. Dave could tell a big difference in his younger mount right from the start. The three of them rode for nearly an hour around the more inaccessible areas of the ranch. Dave was feeling more relaxed as he rode, but a growing case of saddle sores made him more and more uncomfortable. Luckily for him, it was soon noon. They unsaddled the mounts, rubbed them down, and turned them loose in the corral.

The afternoon was busy as Peg showed him around the ranch buildings and acquainted him with the different pieces of equipment. She talked almost constantly, explaining what things were, how this was done, and why this was like it was. Soon it was almost suppertime and Dave was left to his own devices while Peg headed for the kitchen and her mealtime chores.

"What can I do?" Dave asked when he entered the room awhile later.

"Just stay the hell out of my kitchen," Peg responded with a good-natured chuckle.

Dave shrugged, helped himself to coffee, and retired to the ranch office. This small work center separated the living room from Debby's bedroom. In years past, this had been the main entryway to the house. The old front door with its fancy leaded glass panels now was rarely opened. He found the survey map and aerial photos decorating the walls much easier to understand following his daylong tour of the property.

"Time for my story, Dave," a small voice reminded.

Dave looked around, saw Debby waiting with a small book in her hand, and found that he couldn't refuse. They went into the living room together and dropped into the overstuffed chair by the kitchen door. The child crawled up onto the arm and leaned across his shoulders while he began. He read to her, as he had the night before, and from the corner of his eye watched the girl's mother as she added the final touches to their meal. Once again, Peg's call to supper coincided with the end of the story.

The dinner was soon finished and all three of them headed out to take care of their evening chores. Debby looked after the smaller animals while the adults changed the sprinklers. Dave found his saddle sores very uncomfortable as he rode and gritted his teeth, trying to make himself believe that the condition was only a temporary one. With the irrigation lines changed, Peg headed for the kitchen to clean up the mess that had accumulated during the day. While she was busy there Dave milked the cow. He poured an extra gallon of old milk from the cooler into the pigs' bucket and handed Debby a gallon to take to the house. "You carry this one," he suggested. "I'll take the pigs' bucket."

She took the jug in her arms, and they left the barn together. Dave stopped and poured the old milk to the grateful hogs as they passed, and in the twilight, they walked together toward the house. By the time they entered the kitchen, Peg had the room almost presentable. Dave settled down with his coffee and watched television shifting slightly to make room for Debby when she crawled up to perch on the arm of his chair. Peg finished her work and laid down full length on the couch to watch the show.

It wasn't long before Debby fell asleep dropping her head to Dave's shoulder. Peg Martin noticed her daughter several minutes later. "Oh, Debby, come on now," she began, swinging her sock-clad feet to the floor. "You can't sleep there."

With a groan, Peg struggled to her feet, crossed the room, and gathered the child in her arms. Debby threw one arm around her neck and dropped her head onto her mother's shoulder. Peg kissed her lightly on the cheek. "I'll put her to bed, Dave. She's pretty tired."

"I think I'll turn in myself. I'm not used to this way of life yet." Dave squirmed uncomfortably in his chair.

Peg rocked Debby back and forth with a slow twisting motion. "Saddle sore?" she asked with a grin.

"It shows that bad?"

"You look pretty gimpy."

He rose slowly from his chair, a slight flush of embarrassment creeping into his face. "Everything's sore," Dave complained.

"You'll get used to it in a couple of days."

"I hope so. Good night, Peg. I'll see you both in the morning."

"Night, Dave. Sleep well." Peg turned through the office doorway carrying Debby to her room. As they vanished, Dave heard the child's voice muttering and caught Peg's soothing words. The child complained further and Peg's voice rose slightly, emphatically signaling bedtime.

Dave washed out his cup and stepped outside. He walked to the bunkhouse and let himself into the dark room. The first day was always the hardest, he had been told, but he wondered if this was necessarily true.

* * *

Dave's second morning on the Double Bar M started out like his first with the crowing rooster drawing him reluctantly into the new day well ahead of the setting of his clock. He half expected to hear Debby's knock on the door, but the minutes dragged by with no sound. He slipped into his jacket and stepped out into the darkness.

It was twenty till six. Late, Dave thought, for the house to be still dark. He took a short walk around the buildings drawing the crisp morning air into his lungs. Logan saw a light come on in the kitchen and recognized Peg Martin beginning her daily routine. He paused by an ancient ponderosa pine, leaned back against its trunk, and watched while she moved about the lighted room.

Suddenly he felt another touch of indecision like the one he had experienced yesterday. It was a fleeting sense of doubt, almost a warning as he studied her. She was strong, able, intelligent, attractive, and very desirable. The thoughts that yesterday he had shoved deep into his subconscious rose slowly to the surface. He knew and recognized these feelings. He wanted this woman, and there was no denying it. Dave started to think about leaving, before things got out of hand, but then the door burst open, and Debby ran full tilt across the yard heading for the bunkhouse. Dave continued to lean against the tree and let her go right on by.

In the early light of dawn, he watched her pause and knock several times. The child finally opened the door, and a moment later the light flipped on, and then back off almost immediately.

The little girl walked slowly back toward the house the way she had come.

"Hi, Debby," he greeted as she drew abreast of him. "Looking for someone?"

"Oh, hi, Dave!" A broad smile of relief and recognition flooded the child's face. A moment later they entered the house. The aroma of country ham, scrambled eggs, and fresh brewed coffee filled the kitchen. He hung his jacket and cap by the door, and took the cup from Peg's hand.

"Dave was already up," Debby explained.

"At least he's on the ball. I overslept!" Peg confessed.

"What's on the bill for today?" the man asked.

"It's Saturday, and I guess you'd like one day a week off anyway. After we change the lines and milk Elsie, you're on your own. How's that sound?" His employer shoved slices of bread into the toaster.

"Sounds good! I need to get some things in town anyway."

"How about killing two birds with one stone? Take the truck and pick up some grain while you're there."

"OK, glad to!"

"Come on, Spider, lets eat before it's cold," Peg suggested.

"I don't like scrambled eggs."

"Well, that's what you're getting today. Eat them anyway."

They were done with their breakfast in short order, and Peg added coffee to their cups and returned the pot to the stove.

"Dave, did you know Mama has three little fingers?" Debby inquired and, turning to her mother, said, "Show Dave your other little finger, Mama."

"Damn it all, Debby, that's not table talk. How many times do I have to remind you of that?"

"But we're done eating," the child argued.

"He's seen my finger so drop the subject and drink your milk."

There was a moment of uncomfortable silence. Debby pouted and toyed with her glass of milk, Dave sipped quietly at his coffee, and Peg moved pans from the stove to the countertop.

"How long are you going to work for us, Dave?" the child asked.

"A year, I hope," he replied.

"Will you be my daddy after that?" she inquired.

Peg slammed the countertop with her open hand. "Oh my God, Deborah, stop it!" Peg shouted. "I told you last night, drop it!"

A cloud drifted across the cheerful room. Debby sniffed twice and studied her plate carefully, but he could see no tears. Dave tossed down the remainder of his coffee, stroked the child's head in passing, and placed his cup on the counter.

He paused by the woman's side. "Easy, Peg, easy," Dave whispered.

Peg nodded grimly and looked over to where her daughter still sat. "Come on, Spider, get Elsie in. It's getting late," she muttered. Peg's tone was somewhat mellower but still an exasperated tone edged her voice.

* * *

They left the house without further comment. Dave thought that Peg looked tired, and he noted a worried tenseness as well showing in the lines of her face. He remembered her late rising and frowned. From the past heated exchange, he imagined that she had spent a restless night following a lively discussion with her daughter at bedtime. Being a single parent undoubtedly was no easy task.

"Dave, I'll milk. You feed the horses and then saddle ours. When we finish the lines, I'm going up and clean out the strainers up at the creek, so I may not be back quite as soon today."

Logan nodded agreement and went about his chores. He saddled their horses, tied Peg's to the corral fence, mounted his own, and headed down through the field. His head start gave him an edge. He had four lines changed before the woman caught up with him. They finished the work quickly and turned toward their grazing horses.

Logan was puzzled, and he looked at her closely while he gathered up his reins. Peg suddenly appeared much older, her face lined with worry or concern, and she seemed unable to meet his eyes. She made no move toward her reins but pulled off her jacket and draped it across the back of her saddle.

Peg turned to face him. "Dave, it's no good," she began.

"What's no good? What do you mean?"

"It just won't work. You being here is impossible. It's not your work, Dave, you're doing great in that regard; it's Debby."

"What do you mean?" he asked again as he pulled off his jacket and draped it on his saddle horn where the sleeves would dry.

"What the hell, Dave, are you blind? That child is taking to you like a fly to molasses. You should have heard her last night when I went to put her to bed. She wants us to get married! In her mind, you're taking her dad's place. Think of what it will do to her when you leave next spring. By then she'll be so attached that it will literally tear her apart. I saw it happen to her once, and I don't want to see it happen again."

"Maybe I won't be leaving next spring," Dave replied almost surprised at his own statement.

"And just what the hell do you mean by that?" she asked hotly. Before he could reply, she had her own idea. "Wait a minute. I get the picture. You think you've lucked into something here. You see this like some golden opportunity, a ranch up for grabs, a poor widow with no one to look after her." Peg snorted in disgust. "When do you plan to ask me to marry you?" she inquired, pulling off her battered hat and slapping at a bee buzzing around her head.

"Peg, it's not that way."

"I bet! But it really wouldn't matter. There's no community property law in Montana. The ranch goes to Debby regardless, unless I change my will. I've already run off one local cowboy that wanted to put his brand on me. The minute Lou died, here he came all hot to trot. He thought that this was his big chance too."

"Now hold it," Dave exploded angrily. "I've got the resources to buy damn near any ranch I want. I don't need this chunk of ground, and I'm not out to put my brand on some poor widow with her back to the wall. I didn't know your situation when I came out here. You're the one who made that ad up, not me! Don't ever go accusing me of being some land-grabbing fortune seeker, because I'm not." Dave's feelings boiled over at her accusation, and for punctuation he jabbed his finger into her chest at the open neck of her grimy shirt.

Peg forcefully knocked his arm away. "If that's not your plan, what's all this crap about not leaving in the spring?" she asked. "Don't go trying to pull the wool over my eyes; I wasn't born yesterday, you know." I think you've got some rotten motives Colonel Logan."

"Like hell!" Dave laughed openly at her. "I think you're crazy," he alleged. "You said that you hoped for someone younger, some high school kid. You'd have felt nice and secure in that type of arrangement, wouldn't you? When you took me on, were you so dumb that you didn't realize that something might develop between us? I was smart enough to know that you can't coop up two consenting adults together without maybe some feelings developing between them. When I found you were alone here, I almost didn't ask for the job, and just for that reason. After I met you, I figured that you were woman enough to handle it, but I guess I was wrong."

"Hell, you've only been here for two days. What can happen in two days?"

"That was long enough," Dave replied, looking away and nodding.

"Besides, I never thought about it that way at all," Peg argued.

"Not even for a minute?" he asked. "I'll bet." Dave chuckled again in open ridicule.

The woman didn't answer but lowered her head, slightly kicking at the grass at her feet.

"I'll leave, Mrs. Martin, but not because of you. I like Debby a lot, and you're right, it might hurt her a great deal later on if I decided to leave. I wouldn't want to be a part of anything like that. Keep one thing in mind though, and don't you ever forget it. I never had any plans about your ranch or you. I was just smart enough to realize that something might happen between us, just maybe."

Peg looked up at him for the first time in many seconds.

"You're leaving, then?" she said.

"I'll be gone before you get back from the creek. I'll put Goldie up, but then I'm gone. Listen, I'm sorry it didn't work out for you, for us. It's not your fault, Peg, it's mine, really. I don't want to hurt Debby or you. I sure wish both of you the best of everything in the future." Dave turned toward his horse and gathered the reins in his hands.

"Dave, don't go!" Peg hesitated, and then added with a confused toss of her head, "Oh my God, what am I saying?" and she slammed her hat to the ground. Both of their horses spooked slightly at the sudden motion and snorted in alarm.

"I don't know what you're saying," he admitted, steadying his animal and throwing his hands in the air in dismay. "First you want to fire me, and now you're asking me to stay on."

"Dave, you're right. I guess I knew it could happen. I suppose I knew right from the start but didn't want to admit it. Have you ever tried to hang onto something with everything stacked against you? Well I'm trying, and somehow I'll manage with or without you. I've also tried to hold on to a memory, tried to keep Lou fresh in Debby's mind. In that respect, I wasn't succeeding. She felt alone, betrayed, and abandoned until you came. I've never been able to supply all that Debby needs. You brought the first ray of hope that I've seen in her since Lou died three months ago. You woke her up, brought her back to reality, and brought back the old spark. Hell, I'm a mother, Dave, and I want to keep the happiness on Debby's face that resurfaced the day you arrived. I'm a woman too, and damn it all, every woman needs a man."

"But you don't need me!"

"Maybe I do! God knows, Debby does."

Dave turned back to face her. "Just what are you saying, Peg, or trying to say?" he asked.

"Oh, hell, I wish I knew," she admitted, shaking her head. I guess I want you to stay. I want you to be her friend, and God only knows, I need your help. I want to see that smile on her face and the cheerfulness in her eyes, but damn it all you're you, and I'm me. What happens to her if we fail and end up going our separate ways? See, we're back at the same crossroads again," and she bent to retrieve her hat from under her gelding's pawing hooves.

"That's why I think I'd better leave now. I'm not sure it would ever work out."

"I could make it work out, for her sake if nothing more," Peg replied with conviction.

"But why should I want to make it work?" he asked.

"For me, for Debby, and for the ranch."

"Just like that?" he asked, "in that order?"

"You want a ranch? I have one. Debby needs you desperately; we both can see that…Me? Hell, I need a good hand on the place; I need a father figure for my child, and damn it all, Dave, sometimes I need a man too."

"So? What does all that add up to?" Dave asked. "A business proposition, a marriage of convenience, or do we just shack up? What happens to Debby if it still goes to pieces after we've tried?" He gestured helplessly with his hands

"I'll never just sleep with you. It'll be done right, or not at all. It's been only two days, Dave. I won't agree to anything now. Let's just wait awhile and see what develops between us. If it works out for us, I'll marry you, if you'll have me. If it ultimately fails, well by then Debby'll be a little older and hopefully old enough to understand...hopefully."

"Are you saying that you love me?" he asked.

"No, Dave, I can't say that. I'd be lying to you if I did. After all, it's only been two days."

"I must be out of my mind," he replied turning his back on her and swinging aboard his horse.

Peg stepped up to him and placed a restraining hand on his mount's bridle. "Where are you going?" she inquired.

"I'm going to town and get some grain. Hell, lady, I'm as damn crazy as you are!"

"It's a deal then? For now?"

"Peg, you're crazy, you know that? Lou should have called you Spider. You weave a real tight web. I'm not getting married for any reason just yet, but someday it might, just might, work out for us, but I still doubt it. You've got a damn nice ranch here, a real corker of a daughter, and you're one hell of a woman yourself. I sensed it the other day when we first met, and I know it for sure now. I'm willing to give this thing a try."

Peg Martin swung aboard her mount and reined around beside him. "So am I," she replied grimly. "I'll be back shortly. Wait till I get back before you go to town." She kneed her horse forward and swung up the field heading for the distant creek.

They found themselves in a position with no immediate rewards, but at least now the air was clear, with everything out in the open. They knew that there were overlapping goals and strong desires upon which they could try to build a relationship. All of this was complicated by one small life. Debby stood poised between them like a magnet trying to draw them inevitably together. Neither of the adults involved had even an inkling of how it all would end.

As Dave rode back toward the ranch he could see Debby perched high on the corral rails waiting for him. She opened the gate and kept him silent company while he unsaddled his horse.

They walked to the house, and Dave poured the child a glass of milk and settled down with her at the kitchen table to await Peg's return.

She came in shortly, obviously still upset, and without comment moved through the house to the office. She returned to the kitchen and handed two scribbled notes to him. "Pick up this grain at K. C.'s. I'll call them. Just sign the tickets and bring me a copy." Peg handed him the remaining note. "These other things you can get at The Cannery, same deal there. Just sign for them."

"OK, anything else?"

"Nope! Wait, yes! Gas up the truck before you leave. It's almost empty. Gas is in the left tank beside the equipment shed, that's diesel in the right one. Oh, and you better get the stuff on my lists first. Those places both close at noon on Saturdays."

"Is Dave going to town?" Debby asked from her bedroom doorway.

"Yes."

"Can I go?"

"That's up to him, Spider."

"Sure, Debby, come on," Dave replied.

"Brush your hair first and straighten up that room," Peg ordered.

Dave fueled the pickup from the bulk tank beside the shed. He had just finished when Debby came running from the house and climbed into the cab. They waved to Peg while she stood quietly in the doorway, with Wolf at her side, watching them leave.

Even from this distance, he could see the lines of worry and concern in the woman's face. He knew she was deeply troubled and knew too that he was the cause. Still, it was up to her to make the decisions. Dave knew the options that she had decided upon some minutes before were up for review even now. The child beside him was the focal point of the problem. He knew that the choice Peg made would be for Debby's good; she would quickly sacrifice the adult relationships if necessary.

Dave had everything finally checked off Peg's lists. He and Debby had hamburgers for lunch and then spent a leisurely afternoon shopping. It was almost suppertime when they pulled in at the ranch. Dave parked the truck and watched while Debby raced for the door. He entered the house in time to find the child proudly displaying the new cowboy hat that he had bought for her.

"Dave, you didn't need to," Peg said.

He held up his hand. "But I wanted to. I bought myself one too."

Peg smiled, "So I see…Boots too…Come on. Let's eat while it's hot."

Dave saw that the strain was gone from Peg's face. As near as he could tell there were no signs of any of the heated words that had passed between them only hours before.

After supper, they unloaded the grain. Dave was amazed to see that the woman could handle a one hundred-pound sack of feed. She would stand it on end on the open tailgate of the truck, stoop down, and tip the sack over onto her shoulder. The rest was easy. Dave carried the clothes he had bought to the bunkhouse. They milked the cow, finished the minor chores, and changed the irrigation lines. The sun was just setting when they called it quits and headed for the house.

The new was wearing off, and Debby was content to go to bed earlier than she had the first few nights. She was feeling more secure with the knowledge that he would be there in the morning when she awoke. Peg assumed her routine position on the couch watching TV, and Dave retired to the office, picked out a book on cattle, and began to read. He lost track of the time while he studied. Suddenly Peg stepped up to the desk, glanced over his shoulder at the book he was reading, and placed a cup of coffee by his elbow.

"Thanks," he said. "Are your cows likely to get all these diseases?" he asked.

"Thank God, no," she replied with a quiet laugh. "We have enough trouble with the few that are common here. Just read up on these," and she pointed with her maimed finger to the short index list beneath the heavy glass top of the desk.

"Peg, it's none of my business I know, but how did you lose the end of your finger?" he asked.

Peg drew a chair over beside him. "Years ago when I was first roping with Lou I dropped my loop on a big steer. I grabbed the rope wrong when I went to dally, and my finger got caught. Before I could blink, the steer came to the end of the rope and pop, that was that. It didn't cut it off, but it crushed the joint too badly. They tried to save it, but it got infected and had to come off."

"I didn't realize that roping could be so dangerous."

"Oh, it's not bad if you do it right; I just goofed. I'll show you how NOT to lose fingers when we start roping. Don't worry about it."

They discussed cattle and veterinary medicine for some time. Dave sat comfortably in the heavy swivel chair listening while Peg talked. She rocked back casually, on two legs of a straight-backed chair, and crossed her sock-clad feet on the desk top before her. Peg did all her own treating of the stock, except for the most serious of cases. Dave had learned a lot by the time he glanced at his watch and saw that it was already after ten.

"We'd better get to bed," he stated showing her the face of his timepiece.

"It is getting late," she agreed. "And I was up most of last night too, remember?" Peg flipped off the office light, and they moved into the kitchen. She began to wash out their cups in the sink. "I hope you understand about this morning, Dave."

"Yes, I think so."

"While you were gone today, I did some pretty heavy thinking. I guess I'm like you. I knew it could happen, but I never dreamed it would happen so quickly. You know what I mean? Debby liking you so much and coming out of her shell just like that," and she snapped the fingers of her left hand for emphasis. "We're taking a big gamble, you and I, but I frankly like the odds."

Dave nodded slowly. "I think we both learned one important thing today, Peg." There was a long pause before he concluded. "We both have tempers."

Peg nodded in enthusiastic agreement. "And crazy emotions," she added.

Dave smiled in agreement. "Good night, Peg."

"Night, Dave."

She placed her hand on his shoulder and gave him several farewell pats on the back when he turned to leave. While walking to the bunkhouse, Dave glanced over his shoulder just in time to see the kitchen light go off plunging the house into darkness.

* * *

The next day was Sunday and the early morning routine passed quickly. Dave volunteered to clean the head gate strainers and Peg rode back toward the buildings. It had remained quite warm since the first cold morning, and he was becoming accustomed to the saddle beneath him. He found that the horse was proving to be a rather convenient method of transportation after all, not the medieval torture chamber that he had at first envisioned. He was in no hurry and rode slowly while the early sun beat down, shining almost directly into his face. He tipped his new Stetson further over his eyes and soon reached the head gate. Ground reining his horse, he set about cleaning the debris from the screens.

The morning crept on, and sometime later, Dave dismounted by the corral gate and led his mount through. He was undecided when he considered unsaddling, for Peg had mentioned no plans for the rest of the day. Dave led the horse through the other gate and tied him to the tailgate of the pickup near the house.

As he did, Debby came out the door, dressed in clean jeans, a striped jersey, white socks, and Sunday shoes. She dashed past Dave and climbed quickly into the old Volkswagen. Peg followed a moment later her appearance catching him completely off guard. She wore a dark blue straight skirt, open-toed sandals, a long-sleeved white blouse, and no hat. The small handbag that she carried indicated that she was obviously going somewhere.

"We're going to the store and to church, Dave, but there's no hurry. If you want to go we'll wait for you," she invited.

"No. That's OK, Peg. You two just go on," he replied looking the woman over again carefully.

The moderate V neckline of Peg's blouse was clasped firmly together by a small gold pin, (=M). Dave saw too that the small silver studs normally decorating her ear lobes had been replaced by tiny diamonds glistening in a dozen dancing colors in the warm sunlight. Peg had brushed and combed her hair and fastened it back just slightly along the sides of her head allowing the dark auburn waves to fold naturally about her neck and shoulders. She looked nice, and he nodded his secret approval.

"Anything you want me to do while you're gone?"

"No, I try to keep Sundays free. Lord knows, there's enough times in the year when we lose them completely. We'll be back before supper. You can fix your own lunch, can't you?"

"Sure. Say, I'd like to ride up the canyon and look over the cattle, any objections?"

"No, I'd like that; I was going out tomorrow anyway to look them over. Listen, watch for any limping cows favoring a hoof, and keep an eye on the calves for any sign of scouring, you know, diarrhea. If you spot anything like that try and get an ear-tag number we'll doctor them in the morning."

Dave dug into his pocket, pulled out his car keys, and held one out toward Peg. "Here, take my Pontiac. Two girls as beautiful as you deserve better transportation."

"You don't like my bug?" Peg asked pretending to pout.

"I don't like your bug," he admitted shaking his head. "Here, take a good car."

Peg took his keys with a smile. "Thanks. I will," she replied. "Wait till this winter. You'll change your tune when that big limo of yours is stuck in a snow bank, and me and my bug are still going strong."

Dave shrugged her remark aside without comment, knowing that she was probably right, and watched them drive off. He stopped at the bunkhouse, changed his irrigation boots, and returned to his horse. Dave rubbed the animal's nose for a moment, thrust the toe of his new riding boot into the stirrup, and headed up the canyon.

It was nearly an hour before he came across the first of Peg's cows. It stood silently in the shade of a scrub pine chewing its cud, watching him pass. Soon after, he found the bulk of the herd grazing peacefully all across the upper valley. He spotted one of the bulls arduously in pursuit of a cow in heat and with a smile wished him luck. With the exception of the bulls, all the cattle had been dehorned. Calves were everywhere it seemed. He studied them carefully, noting three that he thought were scouring and one lame cow. He jotted down ear-tag numbers of each of the animals needing attention.

Logan headed back down the canyon in midafternoon deciding to ride the irrigation ditch all the way to the south boundary next to the Edwards' place. He reached his goal after a pleasant ride and turning east followed the fence to the cattle guard. Here he turned north and headed uphill along the dirt road heading for home.

He was almost to the top of the ridge when he heard the car coming. He twisted in the saddle and glanced over his shoulder. Dave recognized his Pontiac immediately. Peg slowed to a crawl, and drawing up beside him, leaned out the window. "Where you headed, cowboy?" she asked with a smile.

"Heading home to fix some lunch," Dave replied waving at Debby as he plodded along. From his vantage point atop the horse, he could look down easily into the car. Peg's skirt had slipped up several inches above her knees while she drove. He noted with pleasure that she indeed, had nice legs and forced his eyes aside before she could detect that he was staring.

"I like your new hat and boots," the woman said.

"They're kinda stiff right now, but they'll limber up in a day or so."

"Took me about ten years to get my Stetson broke in where it was comfortable," Peg grinned. "You say you're heading home for lunch? Rather late for that, isn't it?" she asked, glancing ahead at the road briefly.

"Maybe, I didn't wear my watch. What time is it?"

Peg craned her neck from the window and glanced at the sun. "Must be about three, I'd guess." She squinted pretending to measure the sun between her thumb and maimed forefinger. "Make that seven minutes after three," she concluded with a broad grin.

Dave knew that she had seen the clock on the dashboard of his car. "Oh well, supper always did taste better when I was good and hungry."

"I'll see you at the house," Peg answered and slowly increased her speed. Dave waved again at Debby as the car pulled away.

He arrived at the barn some time later and, after entering the corral, he began to unsaddle. Debby ran up from the direction of the house and climbed to the rails of the gate to watch him. The horse had received a long hard workout and was tired, hot, and sweaty. Dave got an old feed sack and a currycomb and began rubbing the animal down.

"How were the cows?" Peg inquired as she rounded the corner of the barn and stopped by the gate to watch him.

"I saw one lame cow and maybe three calves with scours. I've got their numbers written down."

"We'll doctor them in the morning."

Peg had changed into her work clothes, and for the first time these were clean. She had put on fresh Levis, this pair much less faded than the other pair, and a neat cotton shirt, pale rose in color. She still wore her old scuffed boots and dilapidated hat, and he supposed that she always would.

Dave finished rubbing down the mare he had ridden and slipping the bridle off released her. He ducked under the bar in the tack room doorway, hung up the bridle, and turned back. Peg was there leaning across the bar watching him. He caught a flash of white when she turned and saw that several buttons of her shirt were unfastened.

Dave gestured toward his shirtfront and said, "You're unbuttoned...How long will it take to doctor those cows?" he asked.

Peg glanced down quickly, reached up without comment, and buttoned her shirt. "We should be done by noon," she replied "Then we'll change the flood water in some of the lower fields."

"You have to rope the cows to doctor them out there, right?" Dave's words were more of a statement than a question.

"Yes. The calves aren't bad to handle, but the cows are harder. I'll teach you to rope later on, then we can 'head and heel' the cows, that way they're no problem either. That's the way Lou and I handled it. I did the heading and he handled the heeling job. It's tough right now working by myself, but if I'm patient and careful I can even manage the big cows alone."

"How?"

"I heel the critter and let Gus keep everything tight. I sneak up quiet like and give her the shot almost before she knows it. She jumps around quite a bit, but I always manage. With another rider heading the cow we can hold her quite still, even take her down if necessary."

Peg turned away from the bar when Dave ducked under. He fell in beside her as they walked past the barn. He could detect a slight fragrance of perfume for the first time and figured that it was all that remained of her Sunday best.

They were about half way to the house when he placed his hand on her shoulder. He felt her twist just slightly, but she didn't try to shake him loose. A moment later Peg stooped to pick up an old rusty nail from the dirt by the garden fence, and their brief minute of contact ended. They passed Debby swinging happily in her swing by the well house with just a quiet wave. Old Wolf lay close by her side.

Even from out in the yard, Dave could smell chicken roasting. Peg turned to the counter when they entered the kitchen and began putting biscuits together for their supper. Dave poured himself a cup of coffee and retired to the living room. He found the brew too hot to drink for the moment, so he set it aside, and then began sorting magazines. He stacked them neatly according to issue, but the old newspapers he tossed into a separate pile.

He picked up a pair of Debby's old tennis shoes and carried them past the office to her room. The child's room was a shambles, the bed unmade, and toys, books, and clothes scattered everywhere. Dave shrugged, tossed the shoes amid the clutter, and returned to the living room to continue straightening things up.

"What the hell are you doing?" Peg suddenly snapped from the kitchen doorway.

"Just straightening up a little," he replied.

"What are you going to do with those newspapers?"

"Throw them out, I guess. They're all old ones."

"Like hell, you say! There might be something in them that I'd want to clip out." Peg moved fast, gathered the stack protectively into her arms, and then deposited the pile on one of Dave's clean end tables. "I'll sort through them one of these days when I get time," and she turned back without another word toward the kitchen.

Dave shrugged, realizing that she had her ways, probably very set ones. He would have to tolerate some things for now; later he could build her some shelves for her silly newspapers. The shelf would fit well right beneath the front window.

His coffee was cool enough to drink, and Dave moved to the door where he could watch Debby playing in the yard. Peg was still busy in the kitchen with her biscuits. Dave noticed the two white smears of flour across her hips where she had been wiping her hands and he wondered if she even owned a hand towel or an apron.

"Dave! Come swing me," a small voice called from the yard.

"Spider, you just go play. Leave Dave alone, he's tired," Peg ordered.

"That's all right, Peg; I don't mind." Dave finished his cup, shoved it into the clutter of breakfast dishes on the counter, and swung open the screen door. Debby took off for her swing with an excited shout. He swung the child for several minutes and then gave up, dropping to the ground by the base of the big apple tree. Wolf came over and curled up right at Dave's side.

"Come and get it," Peg invited from the doorway moments later.

Dave rose with a groan from his comfortable spot in the shade and started for the house. Debby grabbed his hand and with her short legs tried in vain to measure his stride.

"My legs are way too short, Dave," she complained and releasing his hand, darted for the door. Wolf paced Debby easily, but dropped down by the steps as she scrambled up to the small porch.

Dave stepped into the kitchen and paused to brush the white dusting of flour from Peg's right hip. "A little bit more flour and we could bake you," he said.

Peg shied away from his hand, froze, and glanced quickly at him. She looked at him in a strange sort of way, but then glanced down at her jeans, twisted slightly, and with a daring smile thrust her other hip toward him. He brushed the flour off her pants here as well.

"There," he concluded and gave her a playful slap on the bottom as he turned away.

"Ouch," she cried. "Go sit down, it's all ready."

From the table Debby let loose a happy trickle of laughter, but then she fell silent when Dave placed his finger across his lips in warning. The stillness did little to replace the wide grin of pleasure that the child showed as they began their meal. Sunday supper was over quickly, and it wasn't long before the evening irrigation line changes were complete. The other chores were soon finished as well, and the cool darkness of night began spreading relentlessly across the canyon. Just as full darkness began to set in, a bright full moon rose above the horizon. Dave spotted its glow through the living room window.

"Let's go for a walk in the moonlight," Dave suggested.

There was mutual agreement following his words, and the three of them took a lengthy stroll through the lower fields adjacent to the house. Debby held Dave's left hand tightly while they walked along. Old Wolf walked dutifully in their wake, keeping an eye on what he considered his family.

Dave was very much aware of the tall woman to his right. Now and then, he caught a mere trace of her Sunday perfume, but nothing more. They made no contact during the first twenty minutes of their walk; still she was there close by his side. Eventually they were approaching the house again, and as they neared, Peg slipped her arm through his, adjusting her stride to suit. Their period of contact proved to be short lived, for suddenly they were home, and it was nearly time for bed.

From afar, one could see the lights going out, one by one, room by room, until at last there was nothing except moonlight on the scene. Everyone slept soundly, oblivious to the ceaseless clattering of the sprinkler heads and the whisper of the gentle wind through the trees. The weekend that had started with such a storm had, nevertheless, ended tranquilly and harmoniously for them all.

* * *

Dawn swept over the valley the following day, and they dispensed with their regular chores in short order. Peg called Beth Edwards, warning her that Debby was riding down to spend the day. The child rode off on her old black heading for the Edwards' ranch down the road a few minutes later. Old Wolf trotted dutifully by her side.

Peg packed a bottle of antibiotics, some large medicated boluses, a balling gun, a hypodermic kit, and other items into her saddlebags, and they headed up the canyon. They located the cattle an hour later, and Peg pulled off her jacket, tying it securely behind the saddle. The first ailing animal that they found was a calf, its stained rump indicating obvious scouring.

The woman paused, letting her horse rest. Peg swung her right leg across his neck and hooked her knee around the saddle horn. She rummaged through the saddlebag, slipping several of the large boluses into a shirt pocket and shoved the balling gun under the back of her belt. She pulled a snug-fitting leather glove on to her right hand. In the saddlebag, she located a thin, short length of rather stiff rope and tucked it loosely under her belt over her right hip.

"Just watch how I do it, Dave. Try to remember."

"What's the little rope for?" he asked.

"Piggin' string, for tying the calf's feet. One front and both hind legs. Then I can work on him."

She swung her leg back across the horse, shook out a large loop in her lariat, gathered up her reins, and moved quietly toward the calf. Peg held the coiled lariat and her reins in her left hand. She moved toward the small calf slowly and began swinging her rope over her head.

Dave sat his mount and watched. Suddenly the calf bolted, and through instinct, the horse charged. In two strides, the big gelding closed the gap, and Peg's rope flashed. Peg swung Gus in a quick turn to the left as she dallied in a blur of motion. Peg dismounted on the right side of her mount and was already on the ground when the horse slid to a halt in a shower of dirt. She moved quickly along the taught rope to the struggling calf.

Peg stepped in quickly, leaned across the calf, grabbed the animal by its right flank, threw her right knee under its belly, and jerked him from its feet. The calf was down, and the well-trained horse backed slowly, keeping the rope tight, the calf under control at all times. Peg leaned across the small body, grabbed its right front hoof, threw her right knee down behind the calf's haunches just above his hocks, and with her knee shoved the two rear legs forward. In a flash, she had the piggin' string in place and she tied the calf's three legs. Peg took hold of the taught lariat and called to her horse. "Good boy!" The horse eased forward and Peg threw the loop off the calf's head.

The little steer let out a frightened bawl, and somewhere nearby an alarmed cow bellowed in reply. Peg glanced over her shoulder and yelled, "Keep that cow off me, Dave."

He urged his horse forward between Peg and the worried Hereford. The cow turned aside and stopped to watch. Peg straddled the calf, loaded the balling gun, slipped it down the calf's throat, and passed first one, and then another, of the thumb-sized tablets into place. She shoved the gun back into her belt and stroked the animal's throat for several seconds, helping him swallow. Peg looked the little animal over carefully and then loosened her piggin' string. The calf shook loose, gained his feet, and with a loud bawl raced for his mother's side. Peg swung back aboard her horse, deftly re-coiled her rope, and Dave checked one calf off his list.

"Those cows usually won't bother you," Peg explained, "but they still make me nervous."

"My God, Peg, you're great," Dave shouted excitedly. "Wow!"

"Me? No way! A good puncher would have taken that little guy down in under seven seconds. Probably took me better than thirty."

The second calf was soon located and doctored in the same manner. The dirty rumps of the two calves had stained the front of Peg's jeans, and she wiped at the dirt with an old towel from her saddlebag. Dave spotted the limping cow a half hour later.

Peg rode close to this animal studying it and was finally convinced. "Foot rot, big as hell, right front." Peg dug into her saddlebag again and prepared to give the cow an antibiotic injection. She filled the syringe, flipped the air out of the needle with her finger, replaced the protective cap over the long needle, and took the barrel of the syringe between her teeth.

She quietly shook out her loop and moved in on the cow. It all seemed to happen in slow motion. The cow didn't run, simply limped slowly and painfully away. She swung the rope one time and with a flick of her wrist sent it spinning toward the target. The noose settled vertically, dropped over the cow's hip, and slid down just ahead of the cow's hind legs. The animal took its next step, Peg flipped the noose closed, and dallied fast. The horse backed quickly, almost squatting with his hindquarters to absorb the shock. The cow struggled a moment, then stood rooted, one hind leg stretched uncomfortably out behind.

Peg dismounted normally this time and talked soothingly to the critter as she approached. The cow panicked a little when she neared and struggled even harder. Her well-trained mount met the challenge and kept the rope just tight enough to maintain control.

Peg slapped the cow's rump twice, plunged the needle in, and slowly expelled the medication deep into the muscle. The cow fought slightly all during the procedure, causing Peg to move with agility while she held the needle in place. For several seconds Peg had her hands full as she tried to keep from being knocked down or trampled on by the struggling cow. She finally jerked the needle free, rubbed the area of insertion for a moment, and returned to her horse.

Dave noted that the cow's switching tail had lashed her right across the back, and she came away from the battle with a long dark stain across the back of her clean shirt. He guessed that he'd probably be looking at that streak for many days to come.

"I missed his other leg," Peg complained. "If they're running, they move both hind legs almost together, makes it easier. Walking it's different; they usually move one leg at a time."

As they toured the foothills looking at cattle, Peg explained and demonstrated many of her techniques. Dave unfastened his lariat and began practicing swinging his loop.

"When you dally, always come down on your rope between you and the cow. Never grab the rope with your hand facing upward. That's how I lost this finger. Always dally in a counterclockwise direction. When tying the calf's legs, let your right leg do most of the work shoving the critter's back legs forward against the front leg that you already have in hand. Two good hard turns and then a half hitch is normally enough. They call it 'two wraps and a hooey.'" Peg laughed.

They caught and doctored two other calves during the morning, both without incident. One appeared so docile that Peg let Dave try his hand. Luckily, the calf barely moved, and he was able to drop his loop over its head. Old Goldie took the challenge and held the calf still. Peg dismounted and watched as Dave dumped the calf and bound its legs.

"Guess I set the all-time record with that one." Dave muttered. "That must have been at least a five-minute takedown."

"You did all right. Practice makes perfect."

They found no other animals that needed attention, and it was nearly noon when they headed back for the headquarters.

"Somewhere in the barn we've got an old roping dummy. Lou taught me to rope with it. I'll find it, and you can practice anytime you want."

It had been hot work even in the relative coolness of the high mountain canyon, but it hadn't bothered Dave at all. With the one exception, he had sat comfortably by while Peg had done all the work.

"Next week it'll be your turn," she reminded, wiping a now grimy shirtsleeve across her sweat-streaked face. While Dave studied her, it became apparent that keeping even halfway clean on a ranch was going to be a problem. During his military career, he had become accustomed to changing clothes every morning. Everything always spit and polish. He was beginning to understand why she wore the same grimy clothes day after day. Only hours had passed and the clean clothes that she had put on the evening before already looked like she'd worn them for a week.

It was just past noon when they pulled in and tied their horses by the house. They put away a quick lunch, pulled on their irrigation boots, and headed for the lower fields. Swinging by the equipment shed, they each picked up a long-handled shovel and were ready for work again.

It turned out to be a slow afternoon. Peg showed Dave how to move the small canvas dam from one point to another along the ditch and how to regulate the overflow of water to direct it across the thirsty fields. She managed to get both of her boots full of water before she finally turned the job over to him and settled back in a supervisory role for the rest of the afternoon. Dave was learning slowly, but he was learning.

Peg glanced at the late afternoon sun and called things to a halt. "We'll move the flood in that other field tomorrow, no time for it today."

"If you want, I'll change the sprinklers after supper; and you can change the flood system down here, or vice versa."

"Hey, that's an idea, that way we could finish today like I'd hoped. We'll try it," she agreed.

They picked up their grazing horses and headed for home. While they rode along the ditch, they saw Debby, Sam, and Wolf

THE BEST LAID PLANS OF MICE AND MEN...

plodding up the road far below. She didn't see them until they met at the barn at almost the same time. They tied their mounts to the fence, and Peg headed for the kitchen and the supper chores that awaited her. Debby stayed with the hired man. She chatted with him about her day away from home while he unsaddled and rubbed down her old black. He loosened the cinches of the other mounts and tied them where they were, for they would be needed later on.

As Dave neared the house, he noticed Peg's boots and heavy socks laying out in the sunshine of the yard. He didn't bother to remove his; he had been careful, and his feet were still dry. Dave settled down in a chair by the table while Peg worked barefoot around the kitchen. The legs of her jeans were dark and wet from the knees down, but she didn't seem concerned.

She handed him a cup of coffee. "Do you drink, Dave?" Peg asked.

"Once in a while. Beer mostly, why?"

Peg started peeling potatoes for their supper. "Just wondered, I like one now and then. I'll pick some up next time I'm at the store. One would sure go good right now, but I'm out."

After supper, they went in different directions. Peg rode off toward the lower flood-irrigated field with her shovel, and Dave started on the sprinklers. It seemed an endless task, but finally he was finished. Peg hadn't returned yet so he had Debby bring in the cow and began to milk. He was just washing up the last of the strainers and buckets when the woman arrived.

"How'd it go?" she asked.

"Fine! You fall in again?" he inquired glancing at her boots.

"Nope, not this time. Where's Spider?" she asked.

"I guess she's doing her chores. I haven't seen her since she brought Elsie in."

Peg turned away. "OK. I'll find her."

"Hey, Peg, That lower line, I moved it to the last valve in the main line. What do we do with it tomorrow?"

"Take the Jeep instead of your horse in the morning. Take the pipe trailer down there, load up that whole line, and haul it back up to the top of the field." Peg thought a minute. "I guess take it up to the west side of the main line and start again with it up there at the top."

The following morning Dave did just that. This day pretty much established their routine for the growing season, and in the days and weeks ahead, everything seemed to go about the same. Dave located the roping dummy and tried to spend a few minutes every day, either afoot or on horseback, practicing. Every week Peg had to take time out from the regular ranch work to go to town, do the shopping, wash clothes, and do some baking. While she did these tasks, she kept Dave busy at an endless array of chores: maintaining equipment, fencing, weeding the garden, irrigating, and occasionally doing building repair jobs.

The weather had been perfect, the hay was growing like mad, and their herd's offspring were getting bigger and fatter every week. Peg had spent many hours in their spare time teaching Dave to rope. He was catching on quickly but was far from being an expert. The cattle inspection that they made in early July proved to be his graduation. They found two lame cows and several scouring calves that they doctored on this occasion.

Dave handled all the roping of the calves while Peg administered the medication. When it came to the cows, he and Peg worked as a team for the first time. He snapped his loop into place on the animal's head and Peg dropped hers onto the more difficult target its hind legs. Their two horses held the stretched out cow stationary while Peg gave the needed injections.

In many ways, the ranch operations had evolved into a teamwork undertaking. Dave was holding his own, learning fast, and enjoying his new way of life to the fullest. The grass was almost waist deep in most places, they had about a week to go before they would start haying, and the weather was still holding beautifully. It looked like a good year so far, and Peg was well pleased.

* * *

It was really hot even for mid-July, but Dave had become accustomed to the dry heat of the Montana summer with ease. In the weeks past, the scorching sun had baked his skin to a deep ruddy glow.

The true employer-employee relationship didn't exist anymore, if in reality it ever had. Peg Martin and Dave Logan were more like partners, but not quite genuine in this regard either.

THE BEST LAID PLANS OF MICE AND MEN...

While they went about their daily routine, each of them remembered a half promise made weeks before.

Debby seemed to be the master link in their chain of everyday life. Peg could feel a deep glow of satisfaction, a warm sense of relief, each time she saw the happiness brought to her child by Dave's presence.

They completed a hard day's work, getting the haying equipment ready for use. Supper and the evening routine passed as expected, and at last, Dave retired to his quarters. He didn't know how long he had slept, but suddenly he was awake again.

"Come on, Dave, let's go," Peg ordered as she shook him to full consciousness.

Dave blinked and squinted against the bright light. "What's the matter," he asked sleepily.

"Beth's having trouble with a cow. Come on let's get going!" Peg turned from the room pausing to throw his pants at him as she left.

Dave rose quickly and dressed, noting two in the morning on the face of his clock. He stepped out into the cool of the night and met Peg coming from the direction of the barn carrying a metal tackle box containing her vet equipment. They hurried across the yard to the pickup, climbed in, and headed down the road.

"Debby be all right?" he asked.

"Yes. I woke her up and told her we were going. I left the kitchen light on too."

"What's the matter with the cow?" he inquired sleepily.

Peg explained while they raced along. "Glenn's at a cattle show in Billings. It's their milk cow, it's calving. Beth has been checking and something's not going right."

It was only minutes before they pulled into Glenn Edwards' barnyard. Beth met them and they walked to the barn. Beth was wearing her worn cowboy boots, blue jeans, and her heavy flannel nightgown with its skirt pulled up waist high and knotted about her waist.

"She's been in labor since about eleven, Peg, and isn't making any progress," the older woman explained.

They entered the barn, and in the glow of the few dirty lights, Dave saw the cow. She lay on the straw-covered floor, head stretched flat, obviously in great difficulty. While they watched, the big Holstein stiffened, grunted audibly, and extended one hind leg stiff and straight behind her. One tiny white hoof was visible below the cow's arched tail, but nothing more. The animal relaxed and the shiny hoof slipped back out of sight.

"I'll need a bucket of hot water, Beth," Peg said.

"It's already on the stove." The woman moved quickly out of the barn, and Peg turned to look the facilities over.

"OK, Dave. Let's get her on her feet if we can. I'd rather have her standing if at all possible. We'll put her in the stanchion in that box stall."

Peg spoke to the cow and kicked it gently in the rump several times. It groaned slightly and finally lurched to its feet. It took both of them several minutes to get the reluctant animal into the stall where they wanted it. They finally managed to snap the stanchion shut on her neck just as Beth returned with the steaming bucket of water.

Peg slipped off her jacket and hat, laying them aside on the rail of the stall. She unbuttoned her shirtsleeves and rolled them as far up her arms as she could. Dave saw a deep, eight-inch scar, red, jagged, and ugly, along her left forearm and wondered how that had happened. He suddenly understood why she never rolled up her sleeves even on hot days. Peg opened her vet box, pulled a shoulder-length plastic glove into place on her right hand and arm, and arranged several pieces of equipment in the open lid of the box where they would be readily available.

Peg checked the water temp with her left hand. "OK, Dave. Wash her off real good. Beth, you hang onto her tail for him."

Peg handed him a small scrub brush, and Dave raised the bucket of water behind the cow. Beth grabbed the cow's arched tail and twisted it aside. Dave splashed the cow's rump with hot water and began scrubbing the big Holstein while Peg squeezed a stream of disinfectant soap onto the wet area. She applied more of the lubricating disinfectant the full length of her plastic glove, front and back. Peg finally began splashing water from the bucket onto the cow's rump rinsing the dirty soapsuds away. She added another coating of fresh disinfectant soap.

"OK, Dave. You hold her tail for me now. Keep it twisted tight and push toward her shoulders, that way she can't kick. Beth you hand me things when I need them." Peg muttered softly to the cow as she turned. "Hold still, old girl. Let's see what your problem is."

Dave was fascinated and watched in nervous apprehension while she slipped her fingers into the cow's vagina. He could feel his arms and legs trembling ever so slightly and hoped that neither of the women would notice. Peg's hand disappeared, and the cow humped up while she slowly worked her hand, her forearm, and her elbow deep into the birth canal. Peg chanted soothingly and quietly to the cow. "Sooo Boss, Sooo Boss..." There was a moment's pause. Peg twisted her arm back and forth reaching, searching, probing.

"There's one foot," she muttered almost to herself. There was another long moment of hesitation. "What the hell?" She frowned, a puzzled tone edging her voice. "Hold it, girl, not now." Peg pleaded as the animal grunted and obviously strained again. The cow settled down a moment later and Peg continued.

She plunged her arm deeper, almost to the shoulder. "Oh, OK, here we are," she exclaimed. Her rolled shirtsleeve was pressed tightly against the cow's wet rump, and Dave reached over and tried to shove the sleeve farther up her arm.

"Don't worry about that," she ordered. "He's got one leg back and his head's down." Peg explained the situation grunting and struggling with the twisted calf. She paused and gestured toward the vet box with her free hand. "Give me a short OB chain, Beth."

The woman handed Peg a three-foot length of stainless steel chain with rings in each end. Peg withdrew her arm and fashioned a noose in the end of the chain, like a dog's choke collar. She slipped this over her thumb and carefully re-entered the cow. A long two minutes passed. She cursed several times while she struggled, one-handed and blind, trying to get the chain in place on the calf's ankle.

"Hand puller," she ordered, and Beth handed her the proper tool. Peg hooked this into the chain protruding from the cow's vagina and with her left hand began to pull. "Son of a bitch," she muttered, slacking off and groping again for the elusive leg. She tightened the chain a second time. "There," she exclaimed. "I've got one leg." She pulled the chain tighter, twisting with her right hand and shoulder. Peg worked for several minutes. "There, I've got his head up." Peg sighed with relief. She paused briefly to rest, leaning her head heavily against the cow, using its stained rump for a pillow. Peg finally took a very deep breath. "OK, another chain, Beth. A long one this time. Dave, you hold this one. Keep it snug." Peg passed the hand puller to him, withdrew her gloved hand, and then inserted the second chain as she had the other. Peg worked several anxious minutes before managing to get the second leg pulled up into position.

"OK, Beth, let's have that regular puller of yours now. Keep the chain tight, Dave," she reminded. The woman handed the large mechanical calf puller into the stall, and she maneuvered it into position with the heavy strap across the Holstein's back and the U-shaped crossbar across the back of the cow's thighs below her rump. At the base of the U, a four-foot handle was attached with a small hand winch welded securely in its center. The cable from the puller's small winch was brought forward and hooked snugly into the two O.B chains.

"OK…Dave, you and Beth change places now…Take up the slack…Let Beth have her tail now."

Dave dropped down behind the cow, gripped the end of the calf puller, and cranked the small winch until the cable was snug.

"Hold it right there," Peg warned. "Now, don't crank until she strains. I'll tell you when. When you do start, don't stop unless I say so. Keep cranking no matter what; otherwise she could hip-lock and we'd be in trouble."

"OK," was all Dave managed to say as the tension and excitement of the moment gripped him.

They waited for several minutes, silent except for the deep rhythmic breathing of the laboring cow. Peg's right arm was still deep inside steadying the calf's head. She pleaded with the cow again and again. "Come on, old girl, get with it…Come on now, you're not that tired…Do something even if it's wrong," she begged. "Don't give up on me now!"

Finally, Dave saw the cow stiffen; the animal took a deep breath, arched her back slightly, and grunted aloud.

"OK, now! Crank slow and steady."

He did and watched spellbound while the tightening chains withdrew first one, and then quickly another shiny white hoof.

"Keep the end of the puller down low," Peg cautioned..."Keep him coming...Come on, old girl," she encouraged.

Peg was drawing her arm out slowly while she guided the calf's head upward. Fetal fluid was streaming from the cow, and the calf's legs seemed to grow longer and longer. Peg's right arm and hand slipped free, and the large black muzzle came into view.

Several inches of the calf's tongue were protruding from the corner of its mouth. The calf looked dead to Dave, and for the first time he felt a flash of apprehension and a twinge of doubt.

With an audible groan, the cow forced her calf's head into the world, and the little critter's large wet ears flopped free. Dave was cranking faster now as the tension of the pull decreased. There seemed to be no end to the calf. Peg cradled its head and neck in her left arm, her right poised to catch the long wet body. With a final surge the calf was born. A great gush of bloody fluid followed it into the world, and Peg struggled briefly with an armful of slimy wet calf.

She turned from the cow, quickly carrying the limp newborn out into the main area of the barn. Its umbilical cord pulled free of the cow and trailed after her. Dave removed the calf puller and unfastened it from the chains. Peg gripped the calf's hind legs and hoisted it shoulder high. A large amount of fluid poured from the calf's mouth. She dropped the calf to the straw-covered floor and pried its mouth open, probing deep in its throat for any heavy mucous accumulations. So far the calf had not moved.

Peg picked up a piece of straw and inserted it into the animal's nostril. It twitched one time in aggravation. She slapped him hard across his wet ribs and tickled his nose once more with the straw

The calf snorted, and Dave watched with a sigh of relief as the shiny wet animal's ribs rose for the first time. It shook its head slowly, its huge wet ears flopping comically while a shiver ran the full length of its body. It took another breath, and then another, snorting and wheezing each time. Peg raised a hind leg for a quick look.

"It's a little bull. Go ahead! Turn the old girl loose now!" She removed the OB chains from the calf's front legs and stepped aside.

Dave tripped the stanchion, and the cow backed quickly out. She turned one time and looked at the ground where she had stood sniffing at the large puddle of blood and fluid. The cow bellowed once and looked around the barn in alarm. She spotted her missing calf a moment later, moved quickly to its side, sniffed carefully, and began licking its face almost savagely. The cow's muttering voice was a welcomed sound. They watched while the calf raised its head testing new muscles for the first time. He blinked against the bright light of the dim barn and made his first attempt at rising. He failed.

"He'll be OK," Peg stated as she stripped off the long plastic glove and dropped it into a trash box beside the door. The right thigh of her jeans was soaked and the right sleeve and side of her shirt were too. Pulling a towel out of the vet box, she dried her hands and arms and wiped at the straw and dirt clinging to the wet front of her shirt and pants. Peg rolled her sleeves down and fastened the cuffs. "He'll be all right, Beth. You want to leave them in here tonight?"

"Yes. I'll turn them out in the morning after I give him his shots," the woman replied.

"Let's go home," Peg suggested.

Dave hung Beth's big calf puller on the wall and gathered up their equipment. Peg draped her jacket around her shoulders and, hat in hand, walked to the truck.

"Thanks for everything, Peg," Beth said.

"Hey, anytime. You and Glenn have been up the hill a few times yourselves, remember?"

"Thanks anyway," Beth replied again as she turned and headed across the road toward the lights of her house.

Peg and Dave approached the truck. "You drive," Peg ordered, climbing into the right side.

Dave slipped under the wheel, and they headed home. "I don't see how you did it," he exclaimed shaking his head in the darkness.

Peg laughed. "I didn't see. I felt my way along."

"I mean, how did you know what to do?"

"Well, you read all the books, study all the pictures, watch somebody else once or twice, and then you try. Lou taught me how. I had a smaller hand and arm than he did. That helps.

At times, it's really aggravating. You wish to hell you could get another hand in there, or even one more finger would help sometimes. Come spring, when we start calving, you'll get your share of it, I'll guarantee you that."

"How often do you have to pull them?" Dave asked.

"Oh, maybe one in ten...Oh, maybe not even that often...We watch them carefully. About three hours after true labor begins the placenta may begin to detach itself from the wall of the uterus. When this happens, the calf dies if he hasn't been born. Better to be safe than sorry."

They pulled in by the house and climbed out. The kitchen light was casting a welcoming glow out into the dark yard.

"Bring that box in, Dave," she said. "I need to boil everything we used."

Dave slid the box out of the truck and followed her to the house. He turned to the sink and washed his hands while Peg opened the refrigerator, produced two beers, and nudged the door shut with her hip. She popped the tops and handed one to him. Peg settled herself at the table, and Dave joined her taking a long swig from his can.

"Here's to the new calf," he said raising his beer can in a toast. Peg acknowledged his salute silently, and they sat quietly for nearly a minute. Suddenly Dave grinned and, shaking his head, dropped his gaze to the beer can before him.

"You know? You look like hell," he stated and chuckled quietly.

Peg glanced down at herself and brushed at the damp grimy front of her shirt. It was still covered with hay chaff and dirt and was blood stained in many places. She grinned at him. "Tell you what...I'll do you a favor...I'll put on clean clothes in the morning." She suppressed an open laugh and just chuckled instead. "I guess I do look pretty bad."

"That's an understatement," he said. "You should see your hair."

Peg raised an exploratory hand to the side of her head touching the smear of manure embedded there. "Oh my God," she exclaimed. She rose and quickly headed for the bathroom. Peg flipped on the light and looked at herself in the mirror. "Oh my God, what a mess!"

Peg returned to the kitchen, turned on the water in the sink, and plunged her head under the stream rubbing vigorously at her dirty hair. Groping across the counter, she found the bottle of dish washing liquid and squirted a generous amount onto her wet hair.

"Want some help?" Dave asked moving to her side. "Sure. Scrub it for me."

Dave placed his beer can on the counter and reaching across the woman's back, began to scrub. He worked up a rich lather in seconds, scrubbing hard while Peg groaned with pleasure.

"First lemon-scented shampoo I've ever seen," he said.

"I like lemon," she muttered, her voice sounding hollow from the bottom of the sink.

There was no spray hose in the sink for rinsing, so Dave picked up an empty coffee mug and began rinsing the soap from her hair. It was a lengthy chore, but at last, he was finished. On impulse, he bent down and kissed the back of her wet neck. All time and action hung suspended for one brief moment. There was no sound except for the rattle of the running water in the sink. Then he bent and kissed her neck again.

"Give me a towel, Dave," she directed holding out one hand behind her. He grabbed a large towel from the bathroom and placed it into her waiting hand. Peg wrapped it about her head while still hovering above the drain. Without rising, she swung away from the sink and rubbed hard at the wet hair beneath the towel. She remained bent double while she stood there before him fluffing and drying her hair. Their eyes had yet to meet.

Peg straightened slowly to face him, pulled the towel free, and shook her head casting the wet hair into a mass of confusion. "How's that?" she asked shaking her head again.

Their eyes met and held for a long silent interlude. Suddenly Dave reached for her, gripped both her shoulders firmly, and pulled her quickly toward him. It was a one-sided embrace when their lips met for the first time. Suddenly, Peg's arms circled his neck, and her mouth crushed down hungrily, almost brutally upon his.

Dave's hand slid slowly off her shoulder, across her back, exploring the curve of her spine, the contour of her shoulder blades. He realized that he was in control of this moment and suddenly felt secure

His searching hand passed slowly down her back, circled gently across the firmness of her hip, and inched slowly upward along her side. He could feel the warmth of her body beneath the thin material of her shirt.

They struggled together for a blissful moment. Their world, with a diameter of only six feet, spun crazily around them. Peg dropped her head to his shoulder burying her face for one quiet instant of seclusion. Dave dipped his head, kissing the side of her neck several times, rooting and pushing, trying to shift her face to a more accessible position.

His hand no longer roamed. He caressed the fullness of her breast, gently and firmly, feeling beauty that until then he had only imagined. He turned her face around, and their lips met furiously once more. Her trembling body crushed tightly against him for a fleeting instant.

Suddenly Peg's hands thrust hard against his chest, and she pushed him away. He tried twice to pull her back, surprised each time by the woman's strength as she resisted. She held him at arm's length with their eyes locked for a long, silent, uncertain moment. They were breathing heavily in the stillness of the room. When she started to back away, Dave reached up and gripped her arms restraining her from complete retreat.

Peg shook her head. "Not now, Dave...Please."

He released her with reluctance. Peg shut off the water in the sink and, turning to the table, picked up her beer and drank deeply from the can. He saw her hands tremble slightly and, stepping up behind her, gripped her shoulders again.

"Please, Dave," she begged looking back at him over her shoulder.

"Peg, we're not kids anymore," he protested.

She turned to face him. "I know," she replied. "That's it exactly!"

"What do you mean?"

"I told you once that I'd marry you," she explained.

"Oh," was all Dave could think of saying.

"Listen, it's going to be hard enough on us both. Let's not start out by watching over our shoulders every minute. I don't want to begin with guilt feelings riding us all the time."

"Come on, Peg," he pleaded. "We know what we're doing. We're both adults." He pressed his argument trying again to turn her back into his arms.

"No, Dave! Stop! We're both adults, yes, and I want it to be right, or not at all. It has to be, or there could never be any future for us."

"Damn it, Peg, why?"

"Just because, just because!" She pushed him away with finality. "I guess I'm just too old-fashioned."

There was a long pressing silence. Dave walked to the sink, picked up his beer, and finished it. Peg sat sidesaddle on the edge of the table watching him carefully.

"You want to get married now?" he asked breaking the stillness.

"Yes!" Another very long pause held them, during which Peg slipped from the table, entered the bathroom, and began filling the tub. She returned and leaned back quietly against the doorway.

"I guess we'd better go to town in the morning and get things started then," he added.

"Are you sure, Dave?"

He shrugged. "I'm sure enough to know that I don't want to continue like this."

"It'll be rough, Dave, you and me."

"That's an understatement, I think."

"I'll make it work!" she promised quietly.

Dave corrected her. "Together, we'll make it work!"

Peg shoved herself away from the doorjamb and moved across the room. She stepped up to him cautiously, raised her battered index finger in warning, and kissed him gently one time before turning toward the bath.

"It's almost breakfast time," she reminded, gesturing toward the clock on the stove. "I'm wet, I'm dirty, and I stink! Right now, I'm going to take a bath. We can go to town after the chores are done. God, how I need a bath." She wrinkled her nose at her disgraceful appearance.

THE BEST LAID PLANS OF MICE AND MEN...

Dave nodded in agreement and, with his mind spinning, left the house. He dropped across his bed fully clothed and stared at the dark ceiling, his mind gyrating wildly in a kaleidoscope of realities and dreams.

* * *

Less than an hour later, Dave was startled by a knock on his door. He grunted sleepily and saw Debby's smiling face peek into the dim room. He followed her to the house, still feeling the effects of the long exciting night, and found Peg working over the stove on their breakfast. She had changed clothes but looked tired and worn, far from refreshed.

"Dave didn't undress last night, Mama. He still had his clothes on," Debby stated.

"We just got home a little while ago," Peg explained.

"Grandma Beth's cow have her baby?" the child asked.

"Yes. A little bull." Peg worked her way around the table serving their plates.

"Beth isn't really her grandmother, is she?" Dave asked.

Peg grinned. "No. It's just an honorary title."

They ate in relative quiet and were soon leaving the house for their morning rounds. "Get your work done right off this morning, Spider. We're going to town with Dave after we get done with the chores."

The child let out a whoop and dashed from the house. "I'll get Elsie in," she yelled, and the screen door slammed behind her.

The routine chores seemed endless; both of the adults looked toward the coming day with varying degrees of anxiety and uncertainty. Dave found that Peg had a little influence at the doctor's office. The physician worked them both in between patients, and they were soon on their way. Debby was unaware of the reason for the adults' sudden checkups. They knew there was a three-day waiting period before they could get their license and again before they could marry. They returned home after a brief stop at the store.

The first three days passed quickly, for their fast-paced routine gave them little time to worry about the future. On Friday morning, they headed for Hamilton again and this time stopped at the courthouse. Debby sat quietly on a long bench just inside the clerk's office while her mom and Dave conducted their business at the counter. It was all a quiet formality until they came out of the building and started down the steps on their way back to the car.

"Forty-one years old?" Dave questioned.

"Well. How old did you think I was?" Peg asked.

"Certainly not forty-one. You're old enough to be my mother."

Peg defended herself. "I've got you by only one, that's not so bad."

"I hope you know I'm just kidding," Dave exclaimed.

"You going to have a big service?" he asked trying to talk above Debby's head.

"Not unless you want a big one," Peg replied. "The JP is legal enough for me."

They climbed into the car. "At least we're compatible on that point," he remarked.

All of this discussion slid quietly by above Debby's head. The rest of the morning went quickly by. To an outsider it wouldn't have seemed like there was any monumental occasion looming just over the horizon for either of them. They did a little shopping, bought some needed supplies, and were back at the ranch just after noon. Following lunch, Dave was surprised when Peg dropped to the ground beside him in the shade of the big apple tree.

"Move over, Wolf," she ordered shoving the big dog away. Dave looked quizzically at her. "I just feel lazy," she replied.

Debby climbed into her swing, and Dave rose to give her a shove. Maybe five minutes passed before Peg forcefully suggested that her daughter try riding her tricycle. Debby skipped off, leaving her elders alone in the cool shade.

"Dave, I guess I'd better tell you something else while you're still free to run," Peg began.

"I'm not running!"

"But, maybe you should." She hesitated for long moments, forming her thoughts, choosing her words carefully. "This place is jinxed, Dave. It's bad medicine for everyone who's ever owned it."

"Oh, come on, Peg."

"No! I mean it; it's true! Lou's grandfather was killed when the old barn burned back in the thirties, and right after Lou and I got married, his folks were both killed in a wreck. I was riding with them; that's how I got this bad scar on my arm. Then Lou died way before his time. Hey, it's really something to keep in mind! Just think, three generations."

"Just how did Lou die?" Dave asked.

"He went down to the lower field, below the barn, to check the cows. When they start calving we put them all down there where we can keep an eye on them better. After the calves are born we vaccinate, castrate, and ear-tag them. Then we chase them up into the upper pastures with their mothers where they have many clean, fresh acres to roam on. It was his turn to make the 2:00 a.m. inspection. I woke up at 5:30. Lou hadn't come back. I went to look for him and found him lying beside the Jeep. The motor was running, and the spotlight was focused on a large bloody spot in the snow. He must have come across a cow having her calf and stopped to watch. Coroner said it was a massive heart attack."

"I'm sorry, Peg."

"The hard part is knowing that I slept soundly all through the whole damned thing. If I had awakened sooner and seen that he hadn't come back...Oh, hell...It was just damned hard to take." Silence swallowed them for several minutes. Peg finally shrugged. "Lots of people who owned this place have died before their time."

"Nuts, Peg. I'm not superstitious. I don't buy that stuff about a jinx for one minute," Dave replied.

"I'm not sure that I do either. I just want you to think about it. Don't say I didn't warn you." Peg shrugged off the unpleasant memories and grinned at him while she pushed herself to her feet. She backed into Debby's swing, and without comment Dave moved around behind and gave her several hard pushes. "Whee!" she yelled and finally jumped free. "Come on. Let's get to work," and she raced him across the yard.

The following day was Saturday, and it was another scorcher. They were well behind schedule, and they would be haying by the middle of next week. The normal day off was shoved aside, and after the routine chores were finished they spent the day repairing wooden fence panels that would be placed around the numerous haystacks in the fields. The majority of the crop would be stacked in the fields where it would be more accessible when it came feeding time.

The normal Sunday routine went by the board too, and instead of going to church, Peg turned to the barn. The upper floor had to be ready to receive the baled hay that they fed the horses, bulls, and milk cow during the winter.

"We've got to stack all these old bales from last year over in the front corner so we can use them up first. That way we'll have plenty of room for this year's cutting," Peg explained. "We'll put about thirty tons up here for our immediate needs."

They found the heat in the confines of the hay barn almost stifling. With the sun beating down on the roof, it was like an oven; and Dave knew that it was well over a hundred degrees. They labored for about an hour in the sweltering heat.

"Let's get out of here," Peg gasped, and she slapped her hay hook into the stacked bales and headed for the ladder. She pulled off her gloves and stuffed them into her hip pocket.

Dave didn't argue and followed willingly. Peg reached the ground floor and turned through the barn to the corral. She crossed to the small irrigation ditch where it entered the enclosure, dropped to her knees on the bank, and rocked back resting on her heels. She inhaled deeply in the fresh clean air and, leaning forward, splashed a handful of water onto her burning face.

They were both covered with hay chaff that clung like glue to their sweat-soaked shirts and faces. Dave dropped down beside her and with his bandanna washed the grime and itching chaff from his face and neck.

Peg tossed her hat aside, dropped prone onto the bank, and immersed her entire head in the cool water. She supported herself on one arm, elbow deep in the ditch, while she rubbed and scrubbed at her dirty hair with the other hand.

She rose to her elbows and rested briefly letting the water drain off her face and hair back into the ditch. "God that feels good," she stated.

Dave pulled off his shirt and sloshed it back and forth in the stream, washing the chaff and dirt away. He wrung it out and pulled it back on leaving the wet tails dangling. He found that all this coolness was refreshing, but regrettably short-lived.

"I wish I could do that," Peg remarked.

"Go ahead, I won't look." Dave gestured toward the ditch, throwing her both a dare and a promise.

These she laughingly chose to ignore. "Time to get with it," Peg ordered, and she plunged her head under for a final time.

She grabbed her hat and headed back to the barn sputtering and shaking her dripping head like a wet dog. Peg felt a cool wetness spreading across her back and shoulders from her dripping hair. It felt good, but she knew it would only last for the moment.

It took them the better part of the afternoon to complete their chore, and it was near three when they heaved the final bale onto the stack. Peg hung her hay hook in a bale and dropped down on the chaff-covered floor by the open loft door.

She wiped a grimy wet sleeve across her sweat-streaked face. "Thank God that's over with," she said with a sigh.

Dave sank his hay hook into a bale and dropped down beside her. While they rested in the open door, the air stirred around them feeling cool as it drifted past their hot sweaty faces.

"We'll shovel all this loose chaff out in the morning. I'm too damn tired to worry with it today," Peg said.

"What else you got planned for tomorrow?" Dave asked.

"Just routine, I guess," she replied. "Why?"

"Just wondering. I thought we had some plans."

Peg groaned. "Oh, I almost forgot. I thought I'd be raring to go. Right now all I can think of is a good day of rest." Peg lay back comfortably on the chaff-covered floor, eyes shut tight, hands locked behind her head. "Maybe I'll do just that!" she said.

Dave looked for a long minute at the hot, tired, and dirt-caked woman lying beside him. She looked like hell, but below the grimy surface, he recognized a beauty, charm, and freshness that excited him. Dave realized that he probably looked just as bad himself. He saw the dampness of her shirt and the way it clung temptingly to the curve of her breasts. His gaze traveled slowly down the full length of her body taking in every detail of her inviting form.

"I'm changing your schedule," Dave stated.

"How?" Peg asked her eyes still tightly closed while she rested.

"We'll shovel this mess out today, not in the morning. Tomorrow I don't want anything but routine chores, nothing extra."

"Oh?" she quipped rising to one elbow to look at him.

"That's right!"

Peg grinned at him in a knowing and provocative way. "Why?" she questioned.

"We've got an appointment to keep tomorrow. Remember?"

Peg groaned and rolled over on the hay so that her back was toward him. "I'm going to sleep all day tomorrow," she announced.

"You are like hell," Dave replied. He threw his arm around her waist and rolled her over to face him. When Peg's face came into view, his lips met hers for a brief but rewarding moment.

Peg reached up with the stub of her finger and traced an imaginary line down his forehead to the tip of his nose.

"OK, Dave. I guess I can always sleep tomorrow night."

"Don't count on much sleep then either," he cautioned. Dave drew his finger straight down her face, across her lips and chin, and down farther into the open front of her shirt. He began to slip his fingers inside the damp fabric when she jumped and twisted away from him.

"Behave yourself," she warned. With a playful laugh, Peg dodged out of his reaching arms. "Let's get to work. There's time enough for all that horseplay tomorrow."

* * *

It rained during the night, not much, just enough to kill the dust in the road and dampen the tall stand of hay. A couple of days from now and showers like this wouldn't be appreciated; for they would be cutting, curing, and stacking their hay. Today, however, other thoughts were occupying their minds.

Breakfast slid by, the chores were done, and only their appointment in Hamilton was on the agenda. Dave had completed his work first and had just finished taking his bath when Peg returned to the house. They met by the back door. Dave started to speak, but she stopped him with a raised hand.

"I know what day it is. Don't rush me, OK?" Peg stated this deliberately as she squeezed past him in the narrow doorway.

"That was fun, let's try it again," Dave said as he reached for her arm.

"Oh, behave!" Peg replied shaking herself free.

He shrugged and walked to the bunkhouse without comment.

Dave dressed in his best lightweight suit for the occasion and started back toward the house. Peg met him at the door wearing an old, gray plaid bathrobe.

"Dave, it's unlucky to see the bride before the wedding, don't you know that?" she whispered.

"Not much way around it, is there?" he questioned.

"No, but at least stay out of the house till we get ready to go. All right?"

Dave didn't argue. He walked back to the bunkhouse, settled down at the small table, and tried reading a magazine. It was no use, and he walked outside and paced slowly around the yard, followed closely by Wolf. Suddenly the screen door banged, and he turned to look toward the house.

Debby was running across the yard toward him, and he was startled by her appearance. She wore knee-length white socks, her Sunday shoes, and a frilly blue dress whose puffed sleeves and bouncy full skirt were dotted with tiny flowers of many colors and designs. Her long blond hair was pulled back into a ponytail and tied with a small blue ribbon.

"Oh, Dave," she cried and threw herself into his arms. He caught her and held her close. It was easy to sense the inner joy that held her speechless for a long minute. "Mama just told me, Dave. Are you really going to be my daddy?"

"Yes. In some ways," he replied.

"Wow, now you can call me Spider."

Dave cautioned. "We'll see about that later." He looked to the house as the door squeaked and banged again.

Peg Martin walked across the yard and stopped about ten yards away. She turned around slowly under his appraising eye. Dave rose from Debby's side, still gripping the child's hand, and looked long and hard at the woman before him.

Peg wore a tailored summer dress, long sleeved, and belted snugly at the waist. Her matching yellow pumps made her feet appear tiny after the footwear she traditionally wore. Around her neck hung a single strand of pearls accenting the open V neckline of her dress and glistening white against the dark texture of her exposed skin. She had changed the tiny silver studs in her ears replacing them with her Sunday diamonds. Peg's hair shone glossy and bright as the blazing morning sun added a million highlights to its dark auburn tone. She still wore no makeup that he could detect; in truth, her radiant complexion needed none.

Peg flashed a nervous smile his way. "Will I pass?" she asked.

Dave crossed the open space between them. "You look great," he confessed. He took Peg's arm in his and headed for the car. In minutes, they were on their way headed for Hamilton.

Debby's cheerfulness bubbled, and she was undaunted by the adults' quiet, thought-filled dispositions. As Dave drove, he stole glances at the woman beside him. For the most part, she stared straight ahead, right elbow on the armrest, her chin supported by her clenched fist. He could detect a feeling of apprehension close to the surface and deeper within a sentiment of excitement like his own.

They arrived at the courthouse just before noon. Glenn and Beth Edwards met them just outside the door. Two clerks from the county treasurer's office stood in with them as additional witnesses to the brief ceremony. Debby tried to stand quietly with great dignity, but she only partially succeeded. Before they could catch their breath, Peg had officially become Mrs. Dave Logan.

The trip back to the ranch was as uneventful as the trip to town had been. Becoming husband and wife had done nothing to ease the undercurrent of tenseness that prevailed. If anything, things seemed even more strained than before. Dave parked and they walked toward the house.

Without warning, he scooped his wife into his arms. "Open the door for me, Debby," he instructed.

Wolf let out an audible snarl of warning and moved toward them.

"Down, Wolf, down!" Peg almost shouted. The dog froze and with a degree of uncertainty dropped to his haunches. "Good boy, good boy, you stay now," she warned.

THE BEST LAID PLANS OF MICE AND MEN...

Peg let out a squeal as Dave turned toward the door. The child laughed happily while she held back the screen. Dave kissed Peg lightly and dropped her feet to the kitchen floor.

"OK, Spider, go get those clothes off," Peg stated pointing in the direction of the child's room. "Hang them up too!" she yelled as Debby dashed off.

Dave turned toward the door. "I'm going to change too."

"Wait a minute." Peg caught his arm and turned him back to face her. She glanced toward Debby's room and then gave him another kiss, longer, harder, and with more feeling, than the one a moment before. "Can I ask you a big favor?"

"Sure, name it."

"Take your horse after lunch and go check the cattle."

"Today?" he asked in shocked surprise.

"Please. I've got a lot that I want to get done this afternoon. You'd only be underfoot. Understand?"

"No! Not really."

"It's just this once. I want to have everything just right. Please?"

"Well, OK...I don't feel much like lunch so I'll just head out now and see you for supper.

"Thanks, Dave. I appreciate it." Peg stepped close again and kissed him warmly.

As they broke the kiss and turned away, Dave reached out casually and patted her on the bottom. "Wow, that's nice," he remarked as he started through the doorway.

Peg laughed and aimed a halfhearted kick at him. "Get out of here," she directed as he retreated quickly into the yard.

Dave changed clothes, saddled his horse, and headed up the canyon for an uneventful afternoon. The weather was pleasant even if it was hot, and the cattle were doing fine. In three hours, he had found none that would require any attention.

Peg and her daughter created a whirlwind of activity while he was gone. Peg had changed into her normal comfortable work clothes the finery of the day put safely away for some future important occasion. For the first time in many months, she really cleaned house. The child was a big help as always, carrying trash to the incinerator, dusting, and helping with changing the bedding.

"Throw these out too, Spider," Peg said, and with a sigh of reluctance indicated the huge pile of newspapers on the coffee table.

As the house began to sparkle, she started their evening meal. While the roast cooked, Peg helped her daughter with the table. From deep in her cedar chest, she produced a white tablecloth and from the back of a bottom drawer the few pieces of good silver that she owned. Debby polished two silver candlesticks until she could see her face in them. A fruitless search followed, turning up only one candle in each of several colors. Peg finally decided on a single candle in the center of their festive table. Peg gave Debby the choice of colors, and the child chose red.

As the afternoon wore on, they completed the finishing touches. Peg could feel an excitement building, and she kept looking out across the field watching for the approaching rider. Each time she felt disappointment and the tiniest twinges of worry when she saw only the waving stands of hay.

Finally, Peg spotted him coming, and she heaved an outward sigh of relief. He entered the corral, and she began placing their supper in serving bowls on the table. Dave entered the house a minute later and stopped dead in his tracks.

"Well I'll be!" He looked around in surprise at the tidiness of the kitchen and stepped to the living room door to glance at the picture-perfect room. Everything was neat, clean, polished, and orderly. "You two have sure been busy," he remarked, turning back to face his family. Debby was grinning from ear to ear. Peg's earlier attitude of apprehension had been replaced by an outward sense of calm, satisfaction, and contentment.

They turned toward the waiting meal, and Peg took the seat at the side of the table across from Debby. Dave moved without comment toward the spot she had vacated and slipped into his place at the head of the board.

"You're really my daddy now, aren't you?" Debby asked when he sat down.

There was an uncertain pause. "He sure is," Peg replied.

"In some ways," Dave corrected.

"Then you can call me Spider now, can't you, Dave?" the child asked.

Dave cast a quick look at Peg and noted her brief almost invisible nod. "Hi, Spider," he began. "Come on now. Eat your supper." He smiled while he passed a freshly served plate across to her.

Dave then served his wife and himself and settled down to a marvelous meal, the best he had had in many months. Following supper, Peg immediately began washing the dishes. This was a job that usually wasn't done until after the evening chores and sometimes not even then. Dave watched her for several minutes while he finished his coffee. He finally rose and pulled on his boots.

"I'll get started on the pipes," he stated and turned toward the warmth of the late afternoon. Dave changed all the lines himself and, with a building sense of aggravation, wondered where Peg was and what was taking her so long. When he unsaddled his horse, he noticed that Elsie wasn't in her small field. He turned the mount loose and headed for the barn.

He found Peg just finishing the milking. "I was wondering where you were," he remarked.

"It takes time to clean up after a big meal," she replied.

They moved hand in hand toward the house while darkness began to settle across the valley. The bluffs on the far side of the creek were slipping deeper into shadow, and Debby sat on the steps intently watching the big tomcat eating his evening ration of food. Wolf lay quietly at the foot of the porch steps almost asleep. Peg stopped at the stove to heat up their coffee, and Dave moved to the living room to see what was on TV. He settled down on the couch, which until then had been Peg's exclusive domain. She entered the room shortly, handed him a cup, and relaxed beside him stretching her legs out across the coffee table before her.

"We'll move your things out of the bunkhouse tomorrow, all right?" she asked.

"No hurry."

"I pulled everything off your bed this afternoon."

Dave reached for her hand. "Is that a subtle hint?" he inquired.

"Let's call it an invitation," she replied and snuggled closer.

Debby came in a few minutes later, produced a book, and coaxed Dave into the easy chair for her nightly story. It wasn't long before her nodding head and drooping eyes signaled the end of the day for her, and she turned sleepily toward her room.

Dave moved back to his wife's side on the couch. They were both pretending to watch *Gunsmoke* while Peg snuggled close for the second time. Deep in both their bodies smoldered a desire, a burning need, while closer to the surface they both found a shell of caution, a layer of indecision through which the fire struggled to burn. The long-awaited time was at hand yet they were reluctant to reach out for each other as they had covertly planned for so long.

Peg rose finally, moved through the office to Debby's door, and came back across the room heading for the kitchen. She whispered softly when she passed. "She's asleep. I'll be right back."

Dave sat where he was waiting for what seemed like an eternity. He had almost decided to go and look for her when she returned. Peg reached through the doorway and flipped off the living room light.

For a brief instant the kitchen light behind her cast a warm glow through the smooth flowing blue silk of her gown. It silhouetted the contour of her legs and the graceful curve of her body. Everything it seemed was designed to drive him mad and was well planned to push him far beyond the point of even token resistance.

She crossed to the couch again and eased herself gently down by his side. The flickering glow of the TV screen and the dim light from the kitchen created a relaxed, comfortable atmosphere.

Dave dropped an arm around her shoulders and hugged her tightly. He felt the softness of her gown against his hand and recognized the lingering aroma of her perfume as it slowly surrounded them. Turning to circle her shoulders with both arms, he kissed her tenderly. His hand slid slowly down her arm, across her silk-clad hip, and gently along the warm surface of her thigh.

With quiet determination, Peg slowly unbuttoned his shirt; her fingers caressed the strong muscular body that she had desired for so long. Her kisses danced across his face, and lingered for hungry moments against his lips.

Dave's hand rose across her hip and circled higher along the smooth pathway of silk. There was nothing between his hand

THE BEST LAID PLANS OF MICE AND MEN...

and her beauty except the sheer gown. He kissed her harder this time, trailing his lips slowly along the point of her jaw, down the side of her throat, and deeper into the low V of her neckline.

She rose deliberately, slowly turning her body reluctantly away from his lips. Taking his hand, she urged him to his feet. Dave tried to take her in his arms, but she backed away, leading him, coaxing him, toward the doorway. Peg flipped off the kitchen light as they passed. The bedroom door swung quietly closed behind them and the latch clicked. The forgotten story on the TV tube now glared into an empty and silent room.

* * *

Five thirty the following morning found Peg in the kitchen whipping together a breakfast for her family. She paused in her task to wake Debby. As Peg slid the coffeecake into the oven, the child darted through the room and out the door. A minute or so passed. Peg was just starting the eggs when the little girl returned with a puzzled look on her face.

"Dave's not there, Mama," she exclaimed, her wide eyes asking a very important question.

"Look in there," the woman replied, indicating the master bedroom with a nod of her head.

Debby moved quickly to the door and slipped inside. There was a long moment of silence then Peg heard muffled words, a giggle, and more voices. Debby came back into the kitchen, a broad smile beaming from her face. "I found him, Mama!" she exclaimed victoriously.

Peg smiled at her daughter and again at Dave when he entered the room tucking his shirttails in as he came.

"Hi, beautiful," he greeted. He crossed to Peg's side and gave her a good morning kiss.

"Sit down and eat," she ordered, ducking past his reaching arms with a steaming skillet of scrambled eggs.

Peg set the pan on a hot pad and soon had the rest of their meal together. After they had eaten, she fixed Debby her hot chocolate and refilled Dave's cup.

"What's up for today?" the man asked leaning back comfortably with his coffee.

"How were the cows yesterday?"

"I didn't see a single one that looked like it needed anything."

"Good! I guess we'll pull the water off the fields. The weather reports look good. Shut the water off today, move all the sprinkler lines out, and start cutting tomorrow." Peg stated these plans while she set her dirty plate on the counter.

Dave rose from his chair. "Sounds good to me," he responded. "I'll get started on the milking first."

"OK! I'll go up to the ditch and shut that off," Peg replied. "When you get done milking, get the Ford tractor and the pipe trailer hooked up."

Dave finished milking and turned Elsie loose. He got the tractor out and connected the pipe trailer; he could tell it was going to be a hot day. As Dave drove up through the field, he saw the sprinkler lines going dead as they ran out of water. He reached the uppermost line and began loading sections of pipe on the trailer. Peg came along shortly and helped finish their first load. Back at the barn, Dave waited until she unsaddled and then they unloaded the trailer. They took a break for lunch and by midafternoon found that the fields were clear of pipe.

The three meadows below the road adjoining the creek hadn't had water in several days and they drove down the road in the Jeep to check the condition of the hay. It appeared dry enough to cut and they made their plans to start here in the morning. They had left the Jeep up on the road by the cattle guard and were walking along the lower fence line just above the willows. Peg suddenly crawled between the wire strands, and Dave followed her through the trees down to the creek.

The water was low, but normal for this time of year. She climbed down the bank to a small gravel bar that thrust out into the stream. Peg dropped to her stomach on the warm rocks and took a long drink of the cool water. Dave flopped down beside her and in silence washed his parched face in the coolness of the creek.

Dave glanced at the woman and then turned back for another sip of water. Suddenly Dave felt a strong hand on the back of his neck; and before he could react, Peg shoved his head completely under. The strength in her arms caught him off guard and he called on all his reserves to jerk himself free. He twisted quickly to face her and found her laughing at him. "What was that for?" he asked shaking water from his eyes.

Peg twisted around and sat down cross-legged on the gravel bar beside him. There was a mischievous glint in her eyes.

"Nothing," she replied, and she smiled broadly. She reached out, handing her bandanna to him for a towel.

Dave refused the offer with a shake of his head, pulled his feet under him, and hunkered down before her. Dave looked her straight in the eye and made a prediction. "We're going to do OK, you and me. I just have that feeling."

"I guess time will tell," Peg replied. "It's been a little tough up till now though."

"But last night made up for it. You know, you're a darn good lover, young lady!"

"You don't call a forty-one-year-old 'young lady' without ulterior motives, Dave Logan. What's on your mind?"

"Nothing, honest," he assured, holding his palms upturned before her to show no hidden intent.

The woman rose to her feet with a groan. "I'm glad," she replied.

Peg moved past where he squatted on the gravel bar and in passing swung her knee into his shoulder throwing him off balance. In a flash, she whirled and gave him a shove. Dave had seen it coming at the last instant, and he knew he was going in even before his frantically groping hand closed on her ankle.

Dave hit the shallow water with a splash, and he heard a scream as he jerked Peg's feet from under her. He floundered trying to regain his footing, but still held tight to her one leg. Peg lay flat on her back on the gravel bar laughing at him trying to kick free of his iron grip. Dave began to pull, inching her struggling form across the bar toward the water.

"Oh no! Don't you dare!" Peg yelled. "Dave, don't!" she pleaded.

He slid her closer and closer to the creek. "Come on in," he invited. Peg planted her free foot solidly against a rock in the shallow water. She twisted her body facedown, frantically searching for a secure handhold behind her, but she found none.

With a final heave, Dave tugged her around and dragged her slowly into the stream. She sputtered and gasped when the cold water finally engulfed her.

He released her ankle, and Peg struggled to a sitting position. Dave grabbed her old hat as it drifted by, scooped it full of water, and poured it over her head. Peg sat there in the armpit-deep water sputtering and splashing playfully at him. She finally forced him to retreat. Peg suddenly threw herself forward diving headfirst for Dave's legs.

She caught him perfectly with her dive, and a moment later, they were both almost swimming in the shallow creek. Dave could feel the fullness of her body when she drifted across him. He started to say something, but her lips suddenly found his and speech was impossible. For a long minute, they lay together while the cool swirling water flowed around their bodies. They each felt a surging desire, as their kisses awoke feelings always hidden just below the surface. They floated together for a moment while she fumbled with his heavy belt buckle.

Dave broke the spell as he reluctantly stopped her. He suddenly felt insecure and vulnerable in the openness of the valley. He could feel a million prying eyes staring at him from the surrounding forest. "Come on, Peg, enough of this nonsense. It's getting late."

"Oh, I suppose so," she relented. "You know something? That's one hell of an easy way to do the laundry," Peg remarked.

He turned her loose, and she scrambled wet and dripping out of the creek. Dave slapped her wet rump one time when she passed. "It's fun too," he added, following her to dry land.

Peg grabbed her hat, scrambled up the bank, and, without breaking stride, rolled under the bottom strand of wire. She was on her feet and running before Dave could blink, and he didn't catch up with her until they reached the parked Jeep. He pinned her playfully against the front fender and bent her backward across the hood. Their bodies became community property while they kissed and played for several fun-filled minutes. At last, they separated, and while they caught their breath, they leaned comfortably across the Jeep's warm hood. Minutes later, they surrendered completely and reluctantly headed for home.

THE BEST LAID PLANS OF MICE AND MEN...

Debby was swinging in her swing when they pulled into the yard, and she jumped out and ran to greet them. Peg climbed out of the Jeep and turned to the approaching child. "Hi, Spider. How's my girl?" The child threw her arms around Peg's legs in a big hug.

Debby quickly stepped back, noticing how wet Peg's clothes were. "Mama, you're all wet. What happened?"

"Dave fell in the creek, and I had to rescue him," she lied.

"I heard that," retorted the man still seated in the Jeep. "Don't believe her, Spider. Your mother fell in, and I rescued her."

"Well, if I'd been there I could have throwed you a rope," the child exclaimed.

"I'll bet you could too," Peg agreed. "Come on. Let's get supper started."

Dave watched while the members of his family walked toward the house. He parked the Jeep, entered the kitchen a minute later, and found Peg busy at the sink peeling potatoes. She hadn't changed her clothes yet, and a small puddle of water had run out of her worn boots onto the tile floor.

"You'd better get into something dry," he warned.

"After I get these started. There's no big rush."

Dave shrugged, and entering the bedroom, stripped off his wet things. He dressed, carried his wet clothes to the line behind the house, and hung them out to dry. When he re-entered the kitchen Peg stopped him, leaned toward him carefully, and kissed him lightly.

She grinned at him. "Thanks for helping with the laundry."

"Any time," Dave remarked. "It was fun."

* * *

They cut their first hay the following day, and this started what turned out to be the longest and loneliest period that Dave had spent on the ranch. He drove the small Ford tractor, mowing the tall stands of hay. He worked alone for three days. Peg would come out and relieve him on occasion. After the fallen hay had dried sufficiently, Peg followed with the International tractor pulling the big side-delivery rake. This gathered the fallen hay into fluffy windrows stretching around and around the fields.

They moved field by field, mowing and raking, but rarely working together. The windrows were turned a second time with the rake to complete the drying process.

Finally, Peg dropped her big rake and hooked on to the John Deere hay baler. She eased into the first windrow and at a snail's pace ground her way around the field. Tight, heavy bales of hay dropped to the stubble behind her machine as she moved. At times Dave raised his mowing machine blade and began raking with his tractor. As darkness descended, they flipped on their tractor's lights and plodded on. Several times, they worked until nearly 10:00 p.m.

They met for meals and a few other occasions, but they worked apart. After clearing the hay from a field, they put water back on to start the growing process anew, and with this came the twice-daily irrigation chores again. Peg finally had baled all the hay that she figured they would need. They left these bales where they had fallen until a later date.

She hooked the International onto a hay stacker and began scooping up massive batches of hay. This unit was similar to a front-end loader on a tractor, but was built with long flat tines protruding out in front of the unit. Peg would drive into the end of a windrow with the tines almost tight to the ground and move forward, scooping up a huge mound of hay. She then would raise the tines, drive to a central location in the field and begin stacking. It was quick work overall, much faster than the baling routine.

Finally, the loose hay was all stacked and they loaded and hauled the baled hay back to the barn. The big stacker came in handy here as well. It would lift the small stack of bales right into the high door to the hayloft, almost like a forklift. In the sweltering heat of the barn, they would unload the bales and stack them in the back of the loft. Over the stacks of loose hay in the fields, they spread heavy tarps and erected portable fence panels around the perimeters to keep the cattle out.

They were done by late August and were grateful for a very good season. It had been a tiring period but one with little trouble along the way. Their cattle had been doing well, with no serious problems, and the calves were growing fast. Already they were big, heavy, high-spirited animals that Peg hoped would bring top dollar at the late fall sale. On their recent inspection trips, they had started heading and heeling these big calves, as now they were just too big and ornery to manhandle to the ground.

By early September, the fields were all green and growing again. They shut off the irrigation systems and stowed the sprinkler lines until next spring. They had a few days of steady rain, and then the weather patterns settled in to a few showers now and then.

Their garden had provided for them well during the late summer. With fall coming on they had to preserve the rest of the ripe crop, replenishing their stores for the coming year. The whole family pitched in for the harvest and the days of canning and freezing that lay ahead. For a while, Dave didn't think he would ever get out of the kitchen, but the hard, rewarding task was finally complete.

The freezer in the barn was packed full and the shelves in the pantry behind the kitchen were lined with dozens of jars of produce. They preserved plenty of green beans, sweet corn, green peas, and lima beans. Large crocks held layers of carrots and radishes packed in dry sand. They canned cherries and pears, and made applesauce from their apple trees. All that remained in their garden were pumpkins and several types of squash. They would move these to the cool shelter of the barn in the weeks ahead. Fresh tomatoes were an everyday treat. When the first frosts came, the plants were pulled up carefully and suspended under the barn by their root balls. Here the plants would retain their fruit for many weeks into the cold, inhospitable season.

They winterized the haying equipment and backed the units into the equipment sheds until the following year. They were not irrigating but the fresh stand of new grass was about four inches high, lush, and green, waiting for the hungry herd to come home from their summer grazing lands.

* * *

It snowed twice in the higher elevations in late September, and they knew that they would be bringing their herd in from the hills before long. Today would probably be their last field trip before roundup.

The morning was bright and clear, and by the time the chores were completed it was obvious that it would be a beautiful fall day. Dave saddled their horses while Peg readied her vet equipment for the trip. She called Beth Edwards and found that she and Glenn were on their way to Missoula for the day.

"Can I come with you, Mama?" Debby asked.

"Not today, Spider. We should be back by lunchtime. You and Wolf can hold the fort down for about three hours, can't you? Just stay here and keep an eye on the place for us, OK?"

"All right. I'll put some clean hay in the chickens' nests. They'll like that." Debby smiled and with a wave of her hand turned her back on the corral.

Soon Dave and Peg headed out. By the time they located the first of their animals it was quite warm. Peg tied her jacket behind the saddle and went to work. They doctored two lame cows in the first couple of hours. Foot rot always seemed to be their biggest plague, and with the return of the damp fall weather, it was again making itself known. Several miles up the canyon, Peg suddenly pointed ahead. "There's another gimpy one," she remarked shaking her head and unfastening her rope.

Dave followed suit and swung toward the big Hereford limping ahead of them. He moved in on the cow but never got close. With a quick glance over its shoulder, the cow charged up the canyon.

"That's old number eighteen," Peg yelled. "We'll have a devil of a time catching her. Ought to just let her go."

The two riders worked the excited cow for a half hour trying to haze her into an area that would allow them to rope and treat her. The crafty beast eluded them time after time dodging through the timber and brush just ahead of them. Its swollen hind foot didn't seem to be slowing it down at all. Finally, it ducked into a heavy clump of bushes and turned to stare threateningly at them. The cow panted heavily with white foam flecking its neck and muzzle when it breathed. The cow rested, sensing that they couldn't rope it in the tangle of the thicket.

"I'll circle her, Dave, and drive her out. You snag her when she comes by."

Dave positioned his horse to one side of the copse of trees and shook out his loop.

THE BEST LAID PLANS OF MICE AND MEN...

Peg swung wide around the trees and angled in toward the cow through the brush, trying to haze it into the open. Her horse almost touched the big Hereford before it bolted. In a flash, the cow burst from cover, and Dave charged in behind the big cow. Goldie closed the gap quickly. Ahead Dave saw a small dry wash, perhaps five feet deep and several yards across. He cast his loop, dallied, and hauled back. His horse slid to a grinding stop, and the rope snapped tight. He had her, but it was a battle to hold tension on the cow while it struggled to free itself from his rope.

Peg broke out of the brush and charged in. "Take her, Peg," Dave yelled.

Peg raced up, swung her loop free, and turned toward the cow. When she wheeled in for her throw, Gus stumbled over a small pine log almost hidden in the fallen pine needles and leaves. He scrambled backward, fighting to regain his balance. He almost succeeded, but just as he bunched his feet under him, Peg realized that they had gone too far. The lip of the dry wash crumbled under the horse's hooves. The gelding reared in panic when the ground beneath him fell away, and he squealed in fright, as he started over backward into the shallow depression.

Dave saw Peg try to kick free and in one horrible second saw that it was too late. The horse and rider crashed into the gully in a shower of dust and flying debris. Dave threw off his dally, leaped to the ground, and raced to the edge of the wash. The horse squealed again, its legs thrashing in the air. Then it rolled, gained its feet, and bolted several yards down the ravine.

Dave saw Peg stretch full length in the dirt, roll slowly onto her stomach, and then remain still. He hurried down the bank, tripped and fell, and scrambled on his hands and knees the remaining few yards to her side. Just as he reached her, she turned slowly onto her back again to face him.

"Peg, you all right?" he asked almost dreading her reply.

She made none, but her eyes stared at him with a startled look of surprise. Peg stiffened suddenly, her arms straight at her sides. Dave saw her fingers claw savagely into the ground crushing deeper and deeper into the hard packed soil. Peg's face twisted slowly into a grimace of pain, and her eyes took on an almost inquisitive look. She was breathing fast but shallow, each struggling gasp seeming to shake her entire body.

Dave dug her right hand out of the dirt and felt pain himself when her fingers buried themselves in the flesh of his arm. He tried to raise her arm, but found it stiff and unyielding like a bar of iron. Dave tried in vain to pull free of her clutching hand. "Don't try to move. I'll get some help," he ordered.

Peg's breath rattled noisily in her throat when she tried to speak and then she coughed. Dave watched mutely as her eyes lost the questioning look and stared at him with a mixture of fear and disbelief. Her gasping breath rattled several more times, and she choked again. This time a heavy spurt of dark blood gushed from her mouth. She coughed once more, but this time her breasts failed to rise. A steady trickle of blood flowed from the corner of her mouth; she jerked violently one time and lay still. Her clutching fingers relaxed their frantic grip on his arm, and her hand fell away. Peg's face gradually lost its mask of pain, and Dave saw the anguished look in her eyes slowly fade.

Dave groped at the sides of her throat in desperation, searching for a pulse in her carotid arteries. He could find none. He looked upward through the trees to the towering peak, massive and snowcapped, and glanced down again to the still form beside him.

"My God! Oh my God!" he muttered in disbelief. His head lifted again to the unshadowed majesty of the mountain. "My God, Why?" he screamed. "Why?" Dave's final word, "Why," echoed several times across the stillness of the canyon, thrown back at him in almost a mocking way. He looked down again at the woman's body and gently closed her blank staring eyes. He picked up her battered hat, and placed it over her quiet face.

Dave moved numbly down the wash to her horse, loosened the saddle, and jerked the blanket free. He covered her with the bright plaid material, picked up the reins of her mount, and led the animal out of the wash.

In numb silence, he swung aboard his horse and with Peg's mount in tow, headed down the canyon to make the necessary phone calls. His mind was a blank; he didn't know really where he was, how long he had been riding, or how far it was to the ranch. He shook his head trying to remember.

Gradually his mind swung back to reality. Before him stretched the dark green slopes of the meadows, cool and inviting in the bright October sun. In the distance, he saw the small white house and the cluster of dark red buildings. It was an elegant setting, a place of great beauty.

He suddenly remembered the history of the ranch and the plague of disaster that had seemingly ridden with all of its owners. Yes, it was an elegant setting and a place of great beauty; it was also a fitting stage for terrible tragedy.

He passed through the upper gate and started the slow ride across the field. Below he recognized a small form perched high on the corral fence, and he saw Debby wave.

The grandeur before him suddenly vanished as tears filled his eyes and ran unchecked down his weathered cheeks. He moved with reluctance toward the new owner of the Double Bar M.

* * *

As he neared the gate to the corral, Debby hopped down, ran across, and swung the bars open for him. "Where's Mom?" she asked.

Dave looked quickly away, swung his horse across to the tack room doorway, and stepped down. He jerked the saddle from Peg's mount and just threw it angrily into the tack room. The horse's bridle followed. He was unfastening his saddle when Debby trotted up to him.

"Where's Mom?" she asked again.

Dave dropped to his knees, grabbed the child, and hugged her tightly. Twice he tried to reply, but his voice broke both times. Debby placed her hands on Dave's shoulders and pushed herself back enough that she could look into Dave's eyes. She saw that tears were flowing freely drawing glistening tracks down across the man's dusty weathered cheeks.

"What's happened, Dave?"

The man ducked his head to the child's shoulder for a moment while he steeled his emotions. He finally raised his eyes to meet hers.

"Your mom loved your daddy very much, Debby. Very, very much…She's gone to be with him now."

"But Daddy's dead," the girl replied.

"Yes. I know…Your mother died a little while ago too, and she's with your daddy right now."

The child's eyes flooded with tears. "No!" she whispered shaking her head. "No, Dave, no!"

"Yes, Spider. I'm sorry, but yes."

"Why?"

"Gus fell and hurt her badly. She died a minute later. But it wasn't Gus's fault; it was just a terrible accident."

Dave gently pushed the little girl away, rose, and finished unsaddling his mount. He simply threw his gear into the tack room too. The horse turned out into the corral and trotted across to the small stream of water. During this brief interlude, Debby stood almost silently leaning against the side of the barn. Her shoulders heaved rapidly as her labored breathing shook her body. Tears flowed down her cheeks, but she was not openly crying. Dave wiped his eyes with his shirtsleeve, took the child's hand in his, and walked to the Jeep where it was parked in the shed.

Dave drove quickly down the narrow road. He turned in at the Edwards' place and spotted Beth Edwards, as she moved from the porch toward her parked car. She raised her hand in greeting and tossed her small handbag into the car through the open window.

"Hi there, guys," Beth called.

Dave stopped several yards from the big car. Debby jumped from the Jeep, and with almost a scream raced toward the startled woman. Beth crouched down and caught the child in her open arms, and her anxious gaze settled on Dave's face.

"What's wrong?" she asked.

Debby almost shouted. "Momma's dead, Grandma." She buried her face on Beth's shoulder and sobbed aloud for the first time.

"Dave?" the woman asked searching his face with blank eyes for confirmation or denial.

Dave slipped from the Jeep and just nodded. Beth rose quickly, reached into her car, and sounded the horn with three quick blasts. She waited a moment and blew three more. She picked Debby up and carried her to the porch where she settled down in the big porch swing. Beth cradled the child in her lap while her own tears rolled unchecked down her cheeks.

"Can I use your phone, Beth?" Dave asked.

The woman nodded. Dave entered the unfamiliar house and a moment later located the telephone. He dialed 9-1-1 and with great resolve managed to explain briefly what had happened. He dropped the phone back into its cradle and returned to the porch. Just as he came through the front door, Glenn Edwards wheeled his pickup into the yard and slid to a dust-choked stop right beside Dave's Jeep. He moved quickly to the porch, looked at his grieving wife and the child, and asked, "What's happened?"

"It's Peg Martin," Beth replied. "She's died in an accident!"

Glenn turned to face Dave. "What?"

"We were roping a cow to doctor it. She got too close to a dry wash and her horse slipped and went over backward with her."

"My God. Where is she?"

"Back in the hills still."

"You sure she's dead?"

"Absolutely."

"Have you called anyone?"

"Yes. They're coming."

They sat in stunned silence for several long minutes. Then Dave cocked his head listening. In the distance, he caught the wail of a siren and motioned toward the highway. "Here they come now." He turned to Beth. "Will you keep her for a while?" The woman just nodded.

"I'll go with you, Dave," Glenn said and followed the other down to the Jeep. Dave climbed in and drove the few yards down to the road where he parked. Glenn pulled his makings from his shirt pocket and deftly rolled a cigarette. Glancing over his shoulder, he could see several sets of flashing lights, red, blue, and white, but the scream of sirens had ceased since the small caravan had left the highway. They stopped and a deputy sheriff walked up to the Jeep.

"You Dave Logan?" he asked.

"Yes."

"You called us?"

"Yes."

"We'll just follow you. Can we reach the scene with our cars all right?"

"Have to walk just a little ways."

"OK, you lead out."

The deputy climbed over the spare tire of the Jeep and settled down on the wheel well behind Glenn. Dave took off up the road. As they drove, the deputy asked about the accident and Dave explained all of the facts in detail.

They were soon moving along the maintenance trail beside the irrigation ditch. All the flashing lights had been turned off and everyone in the Jeep was silent. Dave finally veered off the faint trail and began threading his way in and out among the scattered pines. He finally pulled to a stop beside a shallow ravine choked with alder, mountain huckleberries, and other forms of brush.

"I think we can walk the rest of the way easier," Dave announced.

Two search and rescue medics and several deputies gathered their gear, and Dave led off down through the ravine. On the far side, they hiked about a hundred yards through the trees before the landscape opened up before them. Dave saw several of their cattle as they moved along. Suddenly they were there. The group stopped.

"Right over there," Dave pointed.

The two medics hurried across to the edge of the dry wash, paused for a moment, and then scampered down the slope out of sight. Dave led the deputies across the clearing, pointing out just how the scenario had unfolded. The skid marks in the soft ground showed plainly where Dave's horse had stopped after he roped the cow. The sergeant's camera was clicking every so often. He walked to the edge of the wash, photographed the broken edge, and shot repeatedly with his camera aimed down into the depression. He finally climbed down and photographed Peg's body and the surroundings from many angles. Dave went nowhere near the edge of the wash. A handheld radio cracked the stillness, as the medics down below asked for the Stokes stretcher to be brought down. Two deputies carried the stretcher into the wash. A few minutes later, the group struggled out of the depression carrying Peg's body. She had been placed in a dark plastic bag and Gus's saddle blanket, a coiled lariat, and her battered hat rested on the top. Glenn walked up to Dave from the opposite direction and handed him another coiled lariat.

"Found this, Dave, over by those trees. Guess it's yours."

Dave took the rope. "Yes, thanks." Glenn rolled himself a smoke and offered the makings to Dave.

"No thanks, Glenn. Never use it."

Everyone hiked back to the waiting vehicles and again followed Dave's lead, as they wound their way back to the ranch. The deputies opened the two gates and Glenn closed them after everyone had passed through. The chief deputy paused in the driveway of the ranch, while the rest of the small convoy headed down the road. He walked up to Dave, as the Jeep stopped, and extended his hand.

"What can I say, except that I'm so sorry this has happened?" Dave and the officer shook hands. "We'll be in touch with you undoubtedly tomorrow. Her body will be taken to Ridgeway Mortuary in Hamilton, unless you…"

"That will be fine," Dave interrupted.

"Would you like me to notify anyone for you, your minister, some of your kin?"

"Thanks for everything, but no. I'd like to handle this myself. Will you thank the other guys for me?"

The man just nodded, turned to his cruiser, and drove down the road. Dave and Glenn followed. They turned in at the Edwards' place and found Beth still sitting in the porch swing. Debby was nowhere to be seen.

Beth cocked her head toward the house and answered the man's questioning eyes. "She's sleeping, Dave," "You want me to keep her tonight for you? Would that be easier?"

"Yes, if it's not too much trouble."

"No problem at all."

"What about your chores, Dave? You need any help up there?" Glenn asked crushing a spent cigarette under the toe of his boot.

"No. Got to milk the cow and slop the pigs is all, but thanks for the offer. Down the road I'm going to need lots of help, I'm sure." There was a long silent pause. "Thanks for going up there with me, Glenn. I appreciated your company."

Dave left a minute later. It was beginning to get dark when he pulled into the yard. He just left the Jeep in the driveway. He finished stowing all the riding gear from their two horses, milked the cow, and fed the hungry pigs. Old Wolf followed him everywhere he went, undoubtedly wondering where everyone else had gone. Dave decided that he would gather eggs in the morning. It was very dark now except for the single night light high on the utility pole beside the drive.

He was almost to the door of the dark quiet house when he heard a car coming up the road. "Oh no," he thought aloud. "Not now."

The car topped the rise and wheeled into the driveway flooding the area with its bright headlights. He recognized Beth's Oldsmobile as she stopped. The passenger side door opened and Debby slid to the ground. She raced across the dusty drive, and Dave dropped to one knee to catch her as she threw herself into his arms. Beth climbed out of the car, went around to the far side, and closed the open door. She turned to Dave.

"She wanted to be home with you." The woman spoke quietly and then moved back and slid behind the wheel. The door thumped shut and Beth pulled away heading for home.

Dave just waved as the woman passed. He rose, and Debby turned slowly toward the house. As they climbed the few steps to the small porch the little girl asked, "Did you milk Elsie?"

Dave laughed through his tears. "Yes, Spider. I've done it all except for collecting your eggs."

"I'll get them in the morning. All right?"

"That'll be fine."

They entered the house and Dave flipped on the kitchen light. Debby went straight off to the bathroom. When she emerged a moment later, she turned to the door of her mother's room, pushed the door open, and peered into the dark interior. She flipped the light on, and then quickly back off. Closing the door, she walked to the table and quietly sat down.

"Hungry, Debby?" Dave asked.

"No."

"Well we need to eat a little something," he answered. He pulled the fridge door open and began to search. Dave found a small bowl of leftover green beans and a foil-wrapped package of meat loaf. "Ain't much, but it'll do," he remarked.

"Did you feed Wolf?" Debby asked.

"Oh, oh, afraid not," Dave admitted.

The child swung out of her chair. "I'll feed him."

"Supper in just a few minutes," Dave advised.

Their small meal was soon ready. Debby returned and joined Dave at the table. They ate up all the green beans and most of the meat loaf. Not a word was spoken. Dave turned to the sink following the meal and began washing up their few dishes.

"How'd it happen, Dave?" the child asked quietly.

Dave shrugged, turned from the sink, and leaned back against the counter. He reluctantly retraced the events in his mind while he studied the little girl at the table. She seemed to be in complete control, in deep grief no doubt, but in complete control. He started in, outlining the tragic event from the beginning. When he described the crumbling bank and Gus's fall, the child cringed ever so slightly. And when Dave related Peg's last moments, tears welled up in Debby's eyes, and she began to cry, ever so softly. Finally, the tale had been told. Dave picked up the small child and carried her to her bedroom. He snapped on the small bedside lamp and placed her on the bed.

Get ready for bed, OK? I'll be back in a minute to say good night."

Dave finished in the kitchen and turned back to Debby's room several minutes later. The small light was still on; Debby was wearing her flannel nightgown and was tucked snug and warm under one layer of her blankets. She lay face down, her blond head buried in her pillow while she silently cried. Dave dropped onto the bed beside her, lowered his head to her pillow, threw his arm about her shoulders, and began to cry as well. The rooster in the yard woke them both the following morning.

* * *

On this, the first day following Peg's death, Dave found himself faced with tasks that Peg had always done. He used the bathroom facilities and then began uncertainly putting breakfast together. Debby arrived, pulling on her jacket, and without comment slipped out of the house. She returned sometime later carrying her egg bucket.

"Wow! I got sixteen," she announced.

"Want eggs for breakfast or cereal?" Dave inquired.

"Eggs, if you'll fry them for me."

"How you like them?"

"Over easy. That's how Mom fixes them for me sometimes."

"I'll try."

Dave fixed the child's eggs and added toast with jam for good luck. He found a jar of canned pears in the pantry and dished out several slices for each of them. Coffee and fresh milk topped off their meal.

Elsie was milked and the other minor chores put aside. Dave heaved a sigh of relief knowing that he didn't have any irrigation chores to worry about. Peg would have had a list a mile long of things to do today, but Dave returned to the house with his agenda sheet absolutely blank. Blank that is except for the unwelcomed chore of somehow getting a grip on his existence, Debby's future, the future of the ranch, and life as he and the child knew it.

He settled down in the small office and began going through the desk drawers. He found Peg's dog-eared address book and set it aside. In the phone book he found the sheriff's office listing and a number for the mortuary and jotted these down. In the rumpled pages of Peg's listings, he found an entry for an attorney and made a note of this number as well. He paused at one entry titled simply, Mom. The address and phone numbers were in Fargo, North Dakota. Dave glanced at the clock above the desk. It showed 8:30 a.m. He did some quick calculating and found that it was 9:30 in Fargo. Dave hesitated, went to the kitchen, and poured himself another cup of coffee. Back in the office, he dialed the Fargo number.

"Hello."

"Mrs. Gilmore?"

"Yes."

"Dave Logan out here in Montana."

"Oh, hi, Dave good to hear your voice after so long."

THE BEST LAID PLANS OF MICE AND MEN...

"Elaine, I don't know how to say this, but there's been a bad accident out here..." Dave paused slightly letting his words sink in. He heard no response as the distant party waited. He gritted his teeth and plunged ahead. "Elaine, Margaret was killed yesterday afternoon in a horse accident."

There was a scream over the phone. "No!" was the only word he recognized. A clattering crash followed as the instrument was dropped.

"Hello!" The male voice bouncing back sounded urgent, alarmed, and excited. "Who is this?"

"Rudy, this is Dave Logan in Montana, Peg's husband." In the background, Dave could hear the wailing screams of the distraught woman.

"What's going on?" the older man almost yelled.

Dave briefly and quietly explained what had happened.

"The child, Debby, is she all right?"

"Yes, sir. She's fine. She's as OK as can be expected, I guess."

"Have plans been made yet?"

"No, Sir. Ridgeway Mortuary in Hamilton is in charge. I haven't had a chance to talk with them yet."

"We'll be there as quick as we can. Probably drive, so it will be a day or two. Are you all right, Dave?"

"I'm doing OK under the circumstances. I'll manage, and I'll take good care of Debby for you, so don't worry...I'm so sorry." The line suddenly went dead.

Dave was shooting in the dark so to speak, as he called Peg's listings for taxes, and the lawyer. His call to the attorney was a lengthy one. In Peg's will the lawyer had been named executor of her estate. The ball was put in motion immediately. The man recommended that Dave get another attorney to keep from having any conflict of interest problems. Dave found that in Montana, where there were no community property laws, he, as the spouse of the deceased, had no claim to the ranch or any other assets. Debby was the sole beneficiary of the estate with Rudy and Elaine Gilmore, the maternal grandparents, being named as the guardians of the minor child.

A few minutes later, Dave had made an appointment with another lawyer, and had contacted the mortuary with his basic information and instructions. He had just completed these calls when Debby came to the office door.

"The sheriff's here, Dave. He wants to see you."

Dave and the deputy settled down at the kitchen table with mugs of coffee; in detail, Dave spelled out the happenings of the previous day. A small tape recorder recorded his every word.

We'll get this typed out for you, Dave, and send you a copy to sign for us," the deputy explained.

"Whether I sign it, or not, will depend on my lawyer's views," Dave responded.

"I understand." Glenn Edwards arrived just as the deputy was leaving.

He stayed at the ranch all afternoon. The news had spread already. Several other ranchers came by extending their heartfelt sorrow and offering their help at any time. Several women swung by with like messages, and many brought casserole dishes of varying styles to help them with their meals. Dave had not met many of these people, but they had all been close friends with Peg and her late husband. Things settled back almost to normal as the mealtime hour approached. Dave and Debby found themselves alone at last. They milked the cow and tended to the few remaining chores.

Following their great casserole supper, Debby went straight to bed. Dave began poring over documents in the cluttered office. He found Peg's savings account booklet and was surprised to see only a four-digit figure for the balance. Her checking account was not healthy either but was probably adequate for this time of year. They were getting close to market time for their herd, and he knew that the annual income check would swell both accounts to substantial amounts.

Dave didn't worry at all about these documents. He knew that with Peg's death all of the accounts were at least temporarily frozen. His own personal accounts, checking, savings, and securities, were safely in his name only. He could pay the ranch's bills as they came along from his own pocket if need be without any problems. Dave cracked the door to Debby's room and, in the shaft of light spilling in from the office, he saw that she was apparently fast asleep. He snapped off the office light and headed for bed himself.

THE BEST LAID PLANS OF MICE AND MEN...

The man lay quietly for a long time. In his mind, he kept trying to sort out the conditions that had fallen uninvited into his life in the days past. Here he stood with great moral and social obligations. There were no legal requirements binding him, but in the other respects, he felt bound and obligated. On the surface, he was the operator of a Montana cattle ranch, but he had no idea what his next duty should be. He had rough ideas of what lay ahead, but not the faintest degree of expertise to carry out these chores. The herd had to be rounded up and brought down onto the winter grazing fields. Animals had to be sorted, sold, doctored, pregnancy tested, and shipped to market. Winter was coming on and feeding schedules had to be put into place. He had no idea how Peg would have carried out these procedures.

On top of this rode the status of the small child. Debby had lost her father in March and now, just seven months later, her mother as well. She undoubtedly was physically comfortable here on the ranch in the old familiar surroundings that she had always known. She appeared to be deeply attached to him. What was to become of her in the next few days was anyone's guess.

Dave looked at the situation from the opposite angle and found that he had become quite deeply bonded to this little girl. He shook his head in the darkness. The complexity of his situation far surpassed any given moment that he had ever faced during his life. The deep command decisions that he had made while in the Air Force were miniscule in comparison to what he faced today.

* * *

Dawn broke reluctantly on this second full day since the tragedy. It was heavily overcast, with clouds obscuring the lofty peaks off to the west. A light steady rain was falling. Dave took Debby to town after they completed their few chores. He left her in the car while he made a quick visit to the mortuary. In his lawyer's office, the girl sat quietly in the waiting room while behind the closed door Dave listened intently to the possibilities facing him as he viewed his uncertain future. He found that for right now his status was ruled by the whims, decisions, wants, needs, and desires of other people, other agencies, often willing to step in and make rulings for *the good of the child.*

Dave stopped at the grocery in Darby and bought some food. He had no shopping list and had no idea what they were short of. He simply tossed things into his shopping cart that he figured he could prepare without too much trouble. He let Debby pick out several items that she wanted. They drove up the hill and turned into the headquarters. Dave grimaced when he saw the big Chevrolet van parked in the drive. As he pulled in, he noted the North Dakota license and steeled his nerves for the coming engagement.

"That's you grandparents' rig," Dave announced. "Do you know them?"

Debby just shrugged.

As Dave gathered up his bags of groceries, the two visitors came out the door of the house and walked toward him. Wolf walked close by the strangers' side as they approached. Debby stood by the car, uncertain.

"Elaine Gilmore, Rudy, you made good time," Dave began. He glanced at his watch and saw that it was 3:00 p.m.

The older man stepped up and extended a work-worn hand in greeting. He was dressed like any cattleman of the area would have been. "Drove right straight through. Took turns driving. It wasn't too bad. We made it in just under seventeen hours. Good roads this time of year, and all the tourists have gone home." Rudy pulled a pack of cigarettes from his pocket, shook one out, and offered the pack to Dave. Dave declined the offer.

Elaine Gilmore wore cowboy boots, jeans, and a regular Western-style shirt. She had a Levi jacket draped across her shoulders. She knelt down offering her hand to Debby. "You don't remember us very well, do you?"

"I think so," Debby replied as she stepped forward and slipped right into Elaine's arms. "You came when my daddy died," Debby added.

"Yes." The woman hugged her closely. "A couple of times too when you were very young. You sure have grown to be a big girl now."

"Let's go in," Dave suggested, and he turned with his groceries toward the house.

"There's coffee in the pot. Just warm it up a bit," Dave produced two cups from the cabinet and placed them on the table. He unpacked his supplies and shoved the articles into cabinets and the refrigerator.

"That dog of yours…I guess it's a dog…Almost wouldn't let us in the house." Rudy laughed. "Back in March when we were here, Margaret had quite a time explaining us to him."

"That's Wolf," Debby advised. He's half wolf and something else."

For several minutes, they chatted about the trip, the weather, the recent haying season, and the winter to come. "Just what business are you in, Rudy? Peg never mentioned what you did," Dave said.

"Irrigation equipment, farm and ranch supply."

Suddenly Debby turned to Elaine. "Grandma? You want to see my horse?"

The woman hesitated. Dave saw Rudy quickly nod his head to his wife. She took the hint and pushed herself away from the table. The two slipped into their jackets and left the house a moment later. Rudy rose, refilled his coffee cup, and dropped back into his seat.

"OK, Dave. Let's have it," he began. "What happened?"

Dave retold the sordid tale for yet another time. At the conclusion of the story, Rudy leaned back in his chair, looked up toward the ceiling for a minute, and exhaled a long deep breath. He sat upright again and looked Dave right in the eye.

"Don't blame yourself, young man. Things like this happen. Margaret died doing what she loved to do. This was her way of life, her calling. It was all a tragic accident."

"Will you give your wife the details?" Dave asked.

"Yes."

"I'm sorry we couldn't come to your wedding, Dave. It came on quite suddenly, if you remember. Elaine had just gotten over a touch of the flu, and I was right up to here with the business. Whatever…Tell me about yourself, Dave. Margaret told us some, but we don't know much. Where did you come from, and where are you going…particularly now?"

Dave rose from his chair and filled his coffee cup. He threw the old grounds out and began fashioning a fresh pot. He started with his military career, touched on his failed marriage years ago, and explained his plans for his own future that led him to Montana and ultimately to the Double Bar M. He was relating his learning experiences and his work under Peg's guidance when Elaine and Deborah returned.

"That's quite a horse she has," Elaine quipped and winked an eye at Dave.

"Safe and secure for her use," Dave explained.

Debby went back out the door into the yard, and Elaine settled down at the table with the two men. Dave covered the past months here on the ranch, including his marriage to Peg, in the short minutes that followed.

"It was just great. For a couple of weeks we had some very happy times together."

Rudy interrupted and turned to his wife. "I'll tell you about the accident later," he said.

Elaine just nodded.

"Where do you go now, Dave?" Rudy asked as he ground out his cigarette in a jar lid that he was using for an ashtray.

"I really don't know. I love this way of life; and I think I could manage everything, as far as I've been in my on the job training. I know what happens from the end of June until now. But, for the rest of the year I'll be completely at a loss. I really don't know where to turn."

"What you need is a good manager and a couple of good ranch hands. We kept trying to get Margaret to hire someone. She and Lou worked their butts off and made out almost on their own. After his death, she always said she couldn't afford hired help. She was so damned stubborn."

"Opinionated," Elaine cut in.

"Did Margaret change her will at all after you were married?"

"Not that I know of."

"In that case it's probably quite complicated. Everything belongs to Deborah."

"Yes, I know. I talked to Peg's lawyer yesterday."

"Then where do you stand now?" Rudy asked.

"I guess I'm just a hired hand or something like that. Right behind the eight ball mostly."

"I guess we'll be made her guardians," Elaine said.

THE BEST LAID PLANS OF MICE AND MEN...

"That's my understanding," Dave agreed.

Time stood still for all of them as they each tried in vain to grasp an easy way out of the many problems. They searched for some explanation, which would be in everyone's best interest. Such a solution seemed to be beyond their grasp. Rudy finally rose from his chair.

"We can't solve all the problems today. Let's sleep on this for a while. We need to go to the mortuary first thing in the morning and see about the arrangements. Would you like to come with us, Dave?"

"Yes. Right now I'd better start something going for our supper."

Elaine stepped forward, "What can I do, Dave?"

"Well, let's see…"

Together they found what they wanted and began cooking. Debby took her grandfather out to the corral and showed him her prized horse. While they were gone, Dave started to move his things back to the bunkhouse so the Gilmores could have the master bedroom. Elaine stopped this plan in its tracks.

"That's a double bed in the bunkhouse. We've slept there before. It's plenty big enough for the two of us."

"Raining harder," Rudy explained as he reentered the house.

They ate their meal and Debby went to get Elsie. The chores were done soon. While this was happening Elaine washed the supper dishes and cleaned up the kitchen. They all turned in early, as the days on the road had been tiring.

* * *

The following morning, they drove Dave's car and headed for town. The discussions with the mortuary were routine. They all viewed Peg's body. She was young, beautiful, and at peace. She seemed to be only sleeping. Elaine held Debby's hand tightly as the child stared at her mother. Debby reached over, touched her mother, and then began to cry. The open grief spread to the rest of the family. The funeral was set for two days down the road. Dave drove from the mortuary to a small city park beside the Bitterroot River. They all got out and walked along the riverbank while they pulled themselves back together. They visited with

Peg's lawyer and unofficially went over the provisions of Peg's will. It was as they had believed all along.

Peg's funeral brought an outpouring of community sentiments. There was standing room only in the small church. Ranchers, cowboys, loggers, businessmen from all segments of the ranching community crowded the small sanctuary.

Debby held Dave's hand tightly as she looked at her mother for the last time. She pulled Dave down to her level and whispered in his ear. He gathered the small child in his arms and held her over the coffin. Debby bent far down and kissed her mother good-bye. The child's grief was silent, but unchecked tears poured down her cheeks as she walked back to the family's pew. There was not a dry eye in the entire building.

The eulogy and service were brief and heartfelt. Beth Edwards gave a stirring tribute to the young woman who had captured the hearts of the local community with her deep convictions, her faithful resolve, and her great courage in the face of adversity. She spelled out many instances of unselfish dedication to her family and friends. She related several humorous tales that sent chuckles rippling through the sanctuary. When Beth concluded, several ranchers rose and paid many tributes to, what one called, a gallant woman.

The funereal procession to the cemetery must have stretched for over a mile. Most of the vehicles were pickup trucks. Peg was buried in the family plot right beside her husband. When all was said and done, people milled around the memorial park for many minutes. Several ranchers came to Dave.

"I know your herd is still back in the hills. When you're ready let me know. I'll bring my hands, and we'll help you get them in." Many other men sounded this same message, volunteering singly or as a complete outfit.

* * *

They were back at the ranch in the early afternoon. Dave milked Elsie while Debby slopped the hogs and collected her eggs. Elaine fixed their supper, heating up two big casseroles that sympathetic well-wishers had delivered. A woman from Peg's church even brought a cherry pie. While this was going on, Rudy retired to the small office and made one phone call after another.

"Your supper's getting cold," Elaine called as she stepped to the door of the office. Rudy just waved her away, continuing his conversation.

Everyone was done eating by the time Rudy arrived. Elaine dished up his plate and placed it before him. Debby went into the living room and turned on the TV.

"Everything all right back at home?" Elaine asked.

"Fine. No problems. That load of three-inch irrigation pipe has been delayed for maybe two weeks, but we don't need it this time of year anyway."

Elaine nodded. "When we going home?" she asked.

"Thought we'd head back in the morning. Nothing else that we can do here, is there?"

"What about probating Peg's will?" Dave asked.

"We wouldn't have to be here for that. We'll just be notified of any decisions concerning us, and we could appeal if we desired. We all have our lives to live every day, Dave. All this legal wrangling and mumbo jumbo will fall into place eventually without any of us paying any attention to it."

"I hope so," Dave replied.

"I was just talking to..." Rudy began, but faltered.

"Go on...What's on your mind?" Elaine asked.

Rudy hesitated briefly, shook out a cigarette from his pack, and lighted it. "Ed Petron," he began, exhaling a thick cloud of smoke toward the ceiling.

"What about Ed?" she muttered thoughtfully.

"He's one hell of a good hand. Would make Dave a good teacher and helper out here."

"You're kidding?"

"No, really. Ed's folks ran their spread for many years. Ed was raised as a cowboy. He's forgotten more than many punchers today will ever learn. He'd make a darn good ranch hand, and this is just what he's looking for."

Dave listened with keen interest.

"But he's working for you," Elaine reminded.

"I took him on because he couldn't find anything better."

"Joanne too?" she asked.

"Joanne too…And she's damn near as good as he is."

"Careful, Dave," Elaine warned.

"Spell it out for me, Rudy," Dave invited.

"OK…Ed Petron is a top-notch cattleman. His folks are all gone and their ranch has been sold to eastern interests. That was about six or eight years ago. Ed's thirty years old, has a small house trailer that he lives in and travels around taking ranch jobs when he can find them. He was out of work completely, and I took him on last winter. I let him hook up his little trailer behind my warehouse and he works for me hauling equipment and doing other odd jobs. He's very dependable, honest, and hard working. Has two horses that he keeps with him too."

"Rudy, tell him about Joanne," Elaine ordered.

"OK…OK…Ed has a significant other. They aren't married, but they live together. She does odd jobs without being asked. I knew her parents as well. She comes from an old ranch dynasty, kinda the black sheep of the family, but she's a good and steady worker."

"How old is Joanne?" Dave asked.

"She's a child, Dave. She's only sixteen," Elaine cut in.

"Don't look that young to me," Rudy said.

"I take it Joanne goes wherever Ed goes," Dave said.

"That's about it."

"Can she ride?" Dave asked.

"Can she ever…" Elaine chirped. "She's a barrel racer and does great at the fair every year. Has been at it for probably five years now. Started racing as a baby. Good at working cattle too, I hear."

"Were you talking with them just now?" Dave asked.

"Yes."

"Is Ed interested?"

"Yes, but money could be a problem. I'm paying him $300 a month. Not much, but I don't make him pay for his trailer."

Dave thought for a minute. $3,600 a year plus withholding and insurance…"Hey, Rudy. I'm interested. While I'm getting my feet on the ground, I could afford that, at least for one year. You got his phone number?"

"I left it on your desk in there."

"But wait a minute, folks. I may get booted out of her tomorrow."

"Don't see how," Rudy said. We all know what's in Margaret's will. Elaine and I are going to be legally appointed as Debby's guardians. We will hire you as the manager of the ranch. With Ed and Joanne backing you up, I think we'd have a winning proposition. We'll discus your compensation later, but it probably won't be much. The courts will undoubtedly have an accountant going over the books annually to protect Debby's interests."

Dave's mind was in a whirl. So much so that he dared not ask any further questions. "I'll call Ed tomorrow and talk with him."

"The number I left for him is my business number. Just ask for Ed Petron. They'll find him or have him call you back. Right now, there's one major point that we haven't talked about...And this is a tough one, Dave." There was a long pause. Rudy lit another cigarette while Elaine reached across and gripped his hand. The woman began to fidget uncomfortably in her chair.

"To begin with, Dave, I'd like you to try and place yourself in our position..."

"OK, go on."

"We're going to take Debby back to Fargo with us," Rudy announced quietly; he glanced at the child in the living room.

There was utter quiet in the room for close to a minute. Dave turned and glanced at Debby as she lay on the living room floor watching TV. The child had not moved.

"Elaine and I talked long and hard about this last night... Stop and think, Dave. What do we know about you? Really! The child welfare people are sorting through the papers right now. They don't give one hoot in hell about Elaine and me, or about you and the ranch. Their one concern will be Debby's welfare. I'd bet that within forty-eight hours they'll be here to take Debby off to a foster home somewhere, or worse."

"But you folks are her guardians."

"Granted. They would have no legal complaints if the child were living with us. That's why we'll have to take her with us, back to Fargo. To leave her here with almost a total stranger..."

"The bottom line is, you don't trust me alone with your granddaughter," Dave injected.

It was quiet for a moment. "We just don't know you, Dave," Elaine replied. "No one out here does."

Dave slouched back in his chair, beaten, knowing that what they were saying was true. "It will really hurt Debby to take her away from her home, her animals, her way of life. You know that, don't you?"

"We know, but it will only be temporary. She'll adjust. She's going with us, Dave. So don't make it difficult."

"And down the road?" Dave asked.

"When she's older...Maybe summer vacations or the like. I know she'll want to visit her ranch and see how it's coming along."

"Have you told her yet?"

"No."

"You gonna leave early in the morning?" Dave asked.

"Right after breakfast probably."

"I want to pack up some of her things tonight," Elaine added.

"I'll talk to her," Dave said. "I know she'll want to see Beth and Glenn before she leaves. I'll take her down there while you pack up her things."

Dave turned to the living room. "Grab your jacket, Spider. Let's go for a ride," he called.

The child appeared a moment later, glanced at the Gilmores still sitting at the table, and followed Dave out the door. Dave started down the road, and then stopped just out of sight of the house. Dave shut off the engine and the lights. In the darkness, they sat listening to the patter of raindrops on the hood and roof of the truck.

"What is it, Dave?" Debby asked finally.

The discussion that followed was heart wrenching. Dave did his best to explain the legalities of the situation, to show the deep honest concerns of Peg's parents, and he tried to paint a rose-tinted picture of the child's future. All of his words seemed to fall on deaf ears. Debby leaned heavily against him in the darkness crying softly.

They drove down the hill at length and spent nearly an hour with Beth and Glenn. Both people tried to set the child's mind at ease, but they could see that it wasn't working. Debby said her tearful good-byes and she and Dave were back at the house shortly. As they pulled into the yard, they saw Rudy place a large box into the back of his van.

They crossed the yard, entered the house, and Debby turned immediately to her almost empty bedroom. She swung back into the kitchen a moment later and came face-to-face with Elaine as the woman emerged from the bathroom. Rudy entered the room from the porch.

"I don't want to go with you," she said in a very strong level voice.

"It will be hard at first," Elaine said. "But you'll enjoy it after a while."

"Can Wolf come too?"

"I'm afraid not."

"Oh, I hate both of you! Really, I do!" Debby turned silently and went to her room.

"I'm going to bed, guys," Elaine said, swallowing hard as she choked back tears. She slipped into her Levi jacket. "Still raining?" she wondered as she headed for the door.

"Bed sounds good to me," Rudy replied numbly. He ground out a spent smoke and waved to Dave. "See you in the morning."

Dave did not reply to either of them as they left.

The following morning they ate a quick breakfast. Rudy and Elaine sat impatiently in their van with the engine idling. It was still dark when Debby and Dave walked together around the ranch. The child said good-bye to Sam. She brought Elsie into the milk room for the last time and ladled a ration of grain into the feeder for her. She collected her eggs and handed the small container to Dave. He placed it on the ground. Debby hugged Wolf's shaggy neck for long moments. When she started to cry, Dave picked her up and hugged the child tenderly. He carried her to the big van and placed her in the front seat with the Gilmores.

"I'll be back, Dave," Debby promised. They kissed each other, and the door closed.

The Gilmores were gone with the first rays of the rising sun.

* * *

Dave turned back to the barn and with deeply mixed emotions milked the cow. He finished the few chores and went back to the house. Today Glenn Edwards was scheduled to bring his small herd in for their fall roundup. The cattle were all contained in several fields of the property, not on open range, so the roundup chore wouldn't be too difficult. The calves would be separated from their mothers and all would be doctored and vaccinated as necessary. The vet would come in the afternoon to do the pregnancy testing. Before leaving the house, Dave called Fargo and had a lengthy talk with Ed Petron. He also spoke to Joanne Bailey. They reached mutual agreements and the couple would leave right away for the Bitterroot. Dave rode his horse down to the Edwards' place right after completing his chores.

Glenn, Dave, and Beth managed all of the herding. Dave was surprised at what a good horsewoman Beth turned out to be. Finally, all 162 head were safely in the large corral. Beth dismounted, tied her horse to the rails, and watched as the men cut out the two big breed bulls from the lot. Beth, with stock whip in hand, operated the various gates, carefully swinging them open and shut, allowing the animals to be placed into separate enclosures. Glenn worked on foot with a stock whip as the sorting began in earnest. Dave was still on horseback for the most part. He used his coiled lariat to slap and coax stubborn animals along. The calves, one by one, were allowed to escape into an adjacent corral. Their anxious mothers began bawling almost pitifully for their offspring. Before all was sorted out, it was close to noon, and Beth headed for the house to fix their lunch.

The vet arrived on time. The cows were run one by one into the big squeeze chute where they could be held steady. The vet would probe deep into each cow's rectum as he examined the reproductive organs through the thin walls of the intestinal track When the tiny fetus was located the cow would be vaccinated and released into the open field. Glenn had only two open cows. These were each marked with a streak of whitewash across their backs and turned into the same area holding the calves. They were all done by suppertime.

Beth had supper ready when they finished. Dave rode back to the ranch as twilight dropped over the canyon. He unsaddled, cared for his horse, and slopped the hungry hogs. Elsie was milked, the eggs collected, and he settled down in the living room with a bowl of ice cream to watch TV for several minutes.

THE BEST LAID PLANS OF MICE AND MEN...

The phone rang and, after a short conversation, Dave came back to the couch.

The call was from Glenn. He had it all set up where they were going to bring the Double Bar M's cattle in tomorrow. Beth would be coming up to the house to handle the meals."

The following morning, it was still dark when Beth arrived. Dave had just finished his chores. A large pool of light flooded the yard from the standing light on the utility pole, and the floodlight on the side of the barn illuminated the horse corral. Beth brought with her a huge coffee urn and started it percolating right away.

"I've brought some steaks, Dave, to feed the guys afterward," she said.

"I've got plenty too out in the freezer in the milk room," Dave advised. "There's chicken and pork chops out there too."

"I'll wait and see how many there'll be, and I'll get some of yours if I need them."

Glenn arrived a few minutes later on horseback. He tied his mount outside the rails of the corral and joined Dave. Glenn fashioned himself a smoke as he watched Dave working under the glow of the floodlight. Dave finished saddling his horse, led her through the gate, and tied her beside Glenn's mount. Dave called Wolf aside and penned him up, for the time being, in the milk room with his breakfast and a large bowl of water.

Glenn looked toward the sky and saw only darkness. No stars or moonlight could be seen. "Better pack a slicker, Dave. Feels like it might rain. You wear chaps?" he asked.

"Never have."

"Don't like them personally. Lots of the guys do though," the other replied.

Dave rolled his slicker tightly and tied it down behind his saddle. Back in the kitchen, the men helped themselves to cups of coffee from the regular coffee pot. A few minutes passed, and headlights flashed across the kitchen wall as a vehicle pulled into the yard. The first of their helpers had arrived. The pickup towed a large horse trailer.

"Let's open the gate into the field so these guys will have a place to park and unload," Glenn suggested. Before he and Dave reached the gate, another truck pulled up. Glenn waved the drivers toward the big gate, and he and Dave began helping the men unload. Four other rigs pulled into the yard followed by a large stock truck. Dave was amazed at the amount of help that was on hand. Beth was handing out cups of coffee. Four women arrived with their men and began passing out doughnuts from three large boxes.

There were seven trucks in all scattered across the field. The darkness was pushed back by many sets of headlights flooding out across the area and around the yard. It was chilly but not too cold. The big stock truck from the Devons' place carried six horses. The others hauled two apiece. Several empty pickups arrived, carrying men and their equipment.

It was pure bedlam for a while as horses were unloaded. Most were already saddled, but the rigs were checked and everything tightened up for the day ahead. The mounts were tied to the fence rails around the house. Most of the men pulled on heavy chaps over their regular pants. Many of the men paused, attaching spurs to their boot heels. It would be rough going in some places, they knew. Dave watched as two of the women pulled on chaps over their jeans and readied their horses for the ride. Glenn unfolded a survey map from his shirt pocket and whistled for the group's attention.

"Morning, everyone…OK, here it is, guys." Glenn opened the map and held it under the light of a pickup's headlight. The group crowded around. "Here's where we are…I've marked Peg's grazing lease here," he pointed to the dark circled area. Right flank shouldn't have to go any farther than the creek. Left flank scouting up along the rimrock should find them all. Let's split in three groups."

"I'll take the creek side," called one of the men. "I've got two of my boys with me. We'll cover that. I've been in that area too, so I'll find them all right."

From the back of the group a man called, "Hey, Glenn. I worked that rockslide area on the west side last year with Lou and Peg. I know that area."

"OK, Sid. Take a couple of the guys with you. The rest of us will go straight up to the head of the canyon and work our way down."

THE BEST LAID PLANS OF MICE AND MEN...

There was a mutter of agreement and everyone turned toward the horses. The few lights still on in vehicles were switched off; and in the dim light of the coming dawn, the riders prepared to leave.

Without a word, the men began mounting. Eighteen horses milled about the yard, and a slight gray line started to appear over the mountains to the east. Dave and Glenn moved to their own mounts.

Dave swung by the small porch where Beth was standing. "Thank you, Beth," he called.

"Be careful, Dave," the woman replied as he backed his horse away.

Dave and Glenn rode side by side up through the open field. Dave watched as Glenn rolled a cigarette with one hand while his other held the reins. The other riders, sixteen in all, strung out behind. As they crossed through the upper gate onto the Forest Service lands, the group split into three small bands. As Dave rode, he started seeing cattle here and there, but passed them all by.

Before long, they saw no more cows. They rode another half mile and then the group fanned out across the upper reaches of the canyon. The sun had risen, they knew, but had been unable to break through the low layer of heavy clouds. Dave found himself alone. He spotted, and hazed out, two cows and their calves and began pushing them southward down the slope toward home and their winter grazing fields. Occasionally he heard the shouts of men along the line as they pushed animals out of the scrub timber. From near and far, the bellowing call of cattle could be heard.

Dave heard shouts nearby. It sounded like a female voice to him, and he swung slightly aside. He found Nora Devons fighting to get three big cows out of a protecting thicket in which they had tried to hide. Without a word, he swung in and worked with her. Together they managed to push the reluctant animals into the clear. Nora turned back quickly.

"I've got maybe seven more back there," she advised, pointing to the far side of the dense thicket.

Dave swung around with her. Together they persuaded this bunch to join the other. "I've got a few over there," Dave said as he turned away in the opposite direction.

"Thanks for the hand," Nora called as they parted.

Dave located his group and again headed them south. The movement of the cattle seemed to be contagious. Every so often, another cow, usually accompanied by her calf, would slip out of the bushes on her own and join the group moving south.

It was probably almost noon by now. They were about halfway to the ranch and dust was rising in nearly a steady cloud through the trees as group after group merged into one single mass of cattle. It was a stirring sight. Glenn rode up beside Dave.

"How many head does Peg have this year anyway?"

"She said two hundred," Dave replied.

"Quite a bunch, I'd say. Two hundred cows, two hundred calves, a few bulls…There's lots of commotion down by the creek. They've probably got a big bunch down there. I'll go down and give them a hand."

"No way to really count them out here, is there?" Dave questioned.

Glenn pulled back slightly. "Sure, just like they do in North Dakota, count the legs and divide by four," he turned and, with a grin, prodded his horse off toward the timber along the far creek.

As the afternoon progressed, they closed the distance to the gate in the upper fields. The net of riders closed in slowly and cautiously edged the growing herd toward the opening. Cindy Evans worked her big palomino slowly to the front of the herd and began leading the animals along. The cattle in the front of the group followed her. Finally, they spotted the gate and the beckoning grass on the far side of the fence. Cindy swung her horse through the gate and turned quickly aside. The herd began to stream through.

Dave could see that the woman was trying to count as the cattle surged past. Now and then, she stood in her stirrups for a better view as she tallied. A riding quirt dangled from her right wrist and a thin line, probably an old piggin string, was in her fingers. Every so often Cindy would tie a quick knot in this line as she made her count. The riders pulled back allowing the animals to move at their own pace. Finally, they were all in the upper field fanning out, grazing happily on the fresh stand of hay.

THE BEST LAID PLANS OF MICE AND MEN...

"How many did you tally, Cindy?" Glenn asked as he rode through the gate. He stopped and carefully ground out the remains of his cigarette on the horn of his saddle.

"I got 195 cows, best I could count. Didn't try counting calves. May have screwed up a little. You got any makin's left, Glenn?"

Glenn fished his tobacco from his shirt pocked, kneed his horse forward, and passed the packet to the woman. "That sounds about right. Any stragglers will get lonesome back there and come in on their own in a day or so."

Cindy rolled a cigarette and passed the small pouch back to Glenn. She struck a match on the fork of her saddle and inhaled deeply. "I ran out early this morning," she complained.

Glenn waved, turned aside, and rode over to where Dave was. "I'd just leave them all here for the time being," Glenn said as he pulled up. "Lou and Peg usually sorted them out the following day, a few at a time. I'll help you with that phase tomorrow. We won't need all this help for that."

Dave nodded and called the group together. "OK, everybody. I guess we can leave them be for right now. I'll tackle the rest of the job probably tomorrow…What can I say except thanks… Thanks a lot for a big job well done."

"Need any help tomorrow?" one of the men called.

"Glenn says that we'll do it a small bunch at a time. He's going to come up, and I have a man hired who'll be here shortly. We probably won't need any more help right now."

The riders turned and moved toward the ranch. As they drew close, Dave saw smoke rising from the large brick barbecue pit behind the house. Since he had been here, it had never been used.

Beth had found what they needed, and with the help of several other women, and a group of church members, they had the feast well underway. The smell of barbecued steaks and roasting corn drifted on the air. A huge porcelain coffee pot hung from a hook above the sizzling steaks. Two sawhorses and several planks from the shed formed a long table.

The riders paused by the small creek where it flowed along the side of the corral and allowed their mounts to drink. Dave slipped into the corral, unsaddled his horse, rubbed it down briefly, and turned it loose. At the moment, the food was pretty much disregarded, as the other riders tended to their tired mounts. The animals were unsaddled, rubbed down, and had their bridles replaced by comfortable halters. Feedbags were in place on several of the mounts. Only then did the men turn to their own desires.

It was a jovial feast. Men ate and talked, joking about problems they had had during the drive. A keg of beer in the back of one of the pickups drew everyone's attention. Beth's big coffee urn, which had been the focal point of attention earlier in the day, went virtually untouched. The festivities didn't last long, as each of the men there had his own chores to attend to, and there wasn't much daylight left. One by one, the horses were loaded, and the rigs turned down the drive heading for home.

Dave and Glenn sat on the steps of the porch drinking paper cups of beer. Glenn rolled a smoke, and Dave broached a suggestion.

"Let's just let those cattle settle down tomorrow," he said. "I've got a new hired man coming in. Probably get here day after tomorrow. He's supposed to be a darn good hand. I'll call you when he gets here and we can go from there."

It was agreed. Glenn was the last puncher to leave. Beth, and two people from Peg's church, stayed and helped Dave clean up the yard where everyone had eaten. Dave carried bag after bag of trash down to the incinerator and dumped many boxes of edible material into the hog pen. The pigs went wild over the discarded corncobs. For all of the ranch people it had been a long day. Beth left just before dark, and Dave turned to his own chores. He let Wolf out of his prison when he went to milk the cow.

Dave was abed shortly. He tossed and turned, listening to the unfamiliar sound of cattle lowing in the fields. By morning, it was obvious that the herd had located the small creek running along the fence line. Everyone had settled down.

As Dave prepared his breakfast, he went to the door and looked out across the upper fields. He spotted several head of stock huddled close to the gate. He finished his breakfast quickly and, taking the Jeep, drove up through the field and opened the gate for the animals. Without hesitation, the two cows and their calves swung down across the lush green field heading for the rest of the herd.

Before bed that night, Dave went through Peg's supply cabinets in the barn and checked the contents of the small refrigerator in the milk room. He found what he considered an adequate supply of the necessary medications that they would likely need. Ed Petron would be here tomorrow, and Dave knew that he would breathe a lot easier when the burden of operations shifted onto this man's shoulders.

* * *

In midmorning the following day, Dave was sitting on the small porch with Wolf when their hired help arrived. An old Ford pickup towing a small house trailer pulled into the yard followed by a very dilapidated Chevy towing a tandem-axle horse trailer. The horse trailer was in good condition, but the mobile home was obviously quite old and very well used. It was a small trailer, probably twenty-eight feet in length. Protruding from the roof was a four-foot section of stovepipe with its weather cap. The paint on the trailer's walls was blistered and peeling and one small window had been covered by a piece of plywood. In several places along the roofline, Dave could see patches of duct tape holding things together. The beds of both pickups were piled high with an assortment of miscellaneous items.

Dave stayed where he was as the two people climbed out of the trucks. They turned for a moment, slowly looking the headquarters over. The man let go a long streamer of tobacco juice into the grass at the side of the driveway. Wolf let out a deep rumbling growl, and the hairs on the back of his neck bristled slightly.

"It's OK, Wolf," Dave snapped.

The tall, thin man driving the Ford walked across the drive to meet the young girl just opening the back of the horse trailer. She dropped the tailgate, making a ramp, and squeezed inside. A moment later, just as Dave approached, she carefully backed a horse down the short ramp onto solid ground. The man turned to meet Dave.

"Dave Logan?" he asked.

"That's me." Dave replied. I take it you're Ed Petron.

"Guess so. That's Joanne, Joanne Bailey," the other muttered, nodding toward the slim, attractive girl. "Nice looking place you have here. Real sorry 'bout what happened to your wife."

"Thanks…This animal is named Wolf," Dave advised.

"Wonder why they call him that?" Ed muttered with a grin.

"Cause he's half wolf. That's why," Dave replied.

The man nodded. "Where you want me to park this rig?" he asked.

"Follow me."

As they turned away from the driveway, Dave saw Joanne effortlessly vault onto her horse's back. With only a halter in place, she wheeled the small palomino around and rode him bareback down the road at a brisk trot. Dave showed Ed the lay of the land, pointing out several sites that appeared suitable for their small trailer. Ed chose the location behind the house where he could tie into the septic system the easiest.

"It'll be out of sight too from the road, so it won't make your place look too bad," he said with a grin. He spit tobacco juice and used his finger to rake the remnants of the cud from his jaw.

When they returned to the vehicles, they found that Joanne had the second horse unloaded. By the sheer size of this animal, Dave assumed it to be Ed's working mount. The big Appaloosa plunged and reared, but Ed seemed to pay it no heed. Joanne managed to control the animal easily.

"Can I put these guys in the corral with yours, Mr. Logan?" she asked.

"Sure. There's water and feed there too."

The girl gathered up the two halter ropes and led the animals down the long drive beside the barn to the corral.

It took the better part of the day to get the small house trailer in place, blocked up, and connected. Joanne parked the empty horse trailer next to the equipment shed, right beside Peg's big trailer, and came to help with the unloading. By suppertime, the essentials were all in place.

"Want me to fix supper?" Joanne asked.

"Oh no. I'll feed us, but I want to milk my cow first," Dave replied.

THE BEST LAID PLANS OF MICE AND MEN...

Ed followed Dave, and the two talked steadily about the ranch and how, what, and when everything should be done. They continued to talk as Dave milked.

"We need to get those critters sorted out and to market. We wait too long and the price will start to drop. It's a little late in the year, to my thinking, but maybe things are a little slower out here in the mountains. Your calves look like pretty nice animals from what I can see. Should bring a good penny."

Following supper Dave and Ed sat for several hours hammering out what was to be a verbal contract between them. Ed pulled a twist of tobacco from his pocket, bit off a chew, and offered it to his boss. Dave simply shook his head.

Dave found Joanne to be a well-built young woman. She wore her dark brunette hair close cropped about the collar of her shirt. She had a very pretty almost childlike face and wore no makeup or jewelry. She had broad shoulders, narrow hips, log-strong-looking arms and legs, and her hands were chapped and rough. She wore a regular Western-style Stetson low on her forehead where its brim shaded her eyes from the sun. The right side of her hat's brim was curled upward, while the left side turned down toward her collar.

It had been a long day's drive for the two newcomers and they all had put in a hard afternoon's work getting settled. Shortly after supper, Ed and Joanne turned in for the night.

Just after breakfast the following day, two agents of the state welfare agency arrived to take custody of Debby. They were heartened to learn that the child had returned to Fargo, North Dakota, with her legal guardians.

A deputy sheriff that arrived with them gave Dave a copy of the coroner's report. Peg's death had been caused by rupture of the thoracic aorta, that segment of the large artery from the heart above the diaphragm. This was severed by the jagged end of a broken rib forced into the body cavity by the crushing weight of her horse. Another shattered rib had punctured her right lung. The report listed many other broken bones and problems, but there were no head injuries. None of the visitors could shed any light as to when Peg's will was to be probated.

Glenn arrived, and he and Ed discussed the ranch operations for quite a while. For years, Glenn had worked closely with both

Peg and her late husband, so he was well acquainted with the various facilities.

They all swung into high gear the following day. By nightfall the herd had been brought in, the bulls put out to pasture in one of the lower fields, and some of the calves taken away from their mothers. Joanne proved herself an able cowhand all the way. She was a good horsewoman and worked the cattle like a veteran. Beth Edwards was there, lending a hand with the cattle and contributing to the cooking efforts at mealtime. It was sheer bedlam that night, as the bellowing mothers called constantly to their young. It took several days to finish the chore, but, by the end of the week, they had completed the sorting.

The following week livestock haulers appeared on the scene, and the big calves were shipped to the cattle auction company in Hamilton. The vets arrived, and after two long days, the pregnancy testing was completed. Dave had a half dozen open cows that would have to be replaced. Ed singled out one particularly good-looking animal to be slaughtered and packaged for their own use.

By the end of the month, things were almost back to normal. The proceeds from the sale had been rewarding, with Peg's herd bringing second highest dollar for the entire auction. Dave worked closely with Ed on the many chores concerning the cattle, the ranch machinery, and the facilities. He kept a written log, for his own use, of everything that happened, and he made an ongoing effort to keep up Peg's ledgers concerning the ranch's finances.

On one occasion, Joanne invited Dave into her trailer for a cup of coffee. He went with her, cautiously watching for a hint of an ulterior motive. It turned out to be only a very pleasant interval in his busy morning. He was surprised to find the interior of the humble dwelling neat, clean, and orderly. Its furnishings were simple, but appeared very comfortable.

Dave attended to several legal matters along the way as Peg's will was probated. The Gilmores, on Debby's behalf, requested that Dave be given limited power of attorney concerning the operations of the ranch. With the court's permission this was done.

He received one tearful phone call from Debby one evening. He quieted her easily, and they talked for a while about what was

THE BEST LAID PLANS OF MICE AND MEN...

going on. The child was not happy, but was coping to the best of her abilities.

***

Winter descended on the mountain ranch for real in late November. Ed hooked the snowplow up to the big four-wheel-drive pickup. They chained the tractors up, and then they began feeding the herd from the huge stacks of hay in the fields.

One morning, Dave was milking the cow. Ed came and watched until he was done and the cow turned loose.

"Come with me, Dave," the man said.

Dave followed through the lower areas of the barn to the backside of the building adjacent to the open horse corral. Here the horses could get under cover in hot or inclement weather. Ed moved through the small doorway and just stepped aside for Dave to enter. Dave froze. Old Sam lay still on the straw covered floor of the barn, not moving.

"Is he...?" Dave hesitated.

"Died last night sometime," the man replied. "I'll call the rendering plant to come pick him up."

Dave just nodded. That evening he called Fargo and talked with Debby for several minutes. He finally broke down and gave her the news. He could tell that the child was shaken, but she didn't break down as he had expected she would. Her grief would come tonight in the privacy of her own pillow as she remembered her friend.

In late February the first calf was born. The one cow and her newborn were turned loose in the spacious upper field after the calf was ear-tagged. They moved the remainder of the herd to a field just below the barn where they could keep a closer eye on them, watching for any unforeseen problems. The cow and her calf would soon have lots of company. Ed and Joanne spelled Dave checking on the cattle day and night. There were a few problem cases, and Dave finally had his first chance to pull a calf. Ed stayed by his side with a steady run of suggestions. It all turned out perfectly.

Glenn came up, and two other ranchers arrived. They drove the herd into the big holding corral and one by one vaccinated each cow and calf. They branded each of the new calves, castrated the young bulls, and pair by pair turned everyone loose again. At last, it was over. The entire herd was driven out of the upper field to vanish into the open country of the Forest Service lease until next fall.

Dave spared Debby the trauma associated with the slaughter of her two hogs, but he felt obliged to let her know when Wolf vanished on a cold March day. The dog had not eaten his food for two days, but seemed not to be ailing in any known way. Then one morning he was simply gone. He had vanished into the hills to find a secluded den where he would not be disturbed. Debby cried as she received this news.

Spring rolled in across the hills at last. The ditch was opened up. The hay fields were cleared of the remnants of the old haystacks. The stubble of grass was dragged over with huge chain-link sections of fencing weighted down with a layer of old automobile tires. This broke up and distributed the millions of cow pies and helped distribute the nutrients back into the soil. K. & C. Feed Mills tested and fertilized the fields, and the irrigation water was put back onto the ground. Joanne took over the responsibility of flood irrigating the two lower fields, leaving Dave and Ed to handle the sprinkler systems up above. Dave had now been full circle; he breathed easier somewhat, for now he knew what he was doing for a change. He was smart enough to know that he didn't know it all, but Rudy Gilmore had been right. Ed Petron was a great teacher, and every day Dave learned many important details about each of the ranch's operations.

The days turned to weeks, the weeks to months, and time surged relentlessly forward. Dave ate at a small restaurant in Darby now and then and soon developed a friendly relationship with the owner of the establishment. On several occasions, Saturday night dances brought fun-filled interludes into Dave's life.

Suddenly he realized that it had been over a year. Then he flipped over the October calendar sheet and stared at November 1972. The fifteenth of the month was circled in red, Debby's birthday. She would now be turning eight.

Dave boarded a plane in Missoula and hours later landed in Fargo. The surprise birthday party went all wrong. Debby was a big, tall, beautiful, young girl and was simply overjoyed to see Dave after a long two years apart.

"You've come to take me home?" she asked immediately.

That was the end of the happy birthday party. All of the animosity was covertly directed at the poor grandparents. Dave and the Gilmores held a long discussion that night. Debby was a good girl. However, she refused to settle down in school. Her grades were very poor except for reading. She was an obedient child never openly causing any trouble, but she was hostile and cantankerous in a compulsive and hard-to-understand manner.

"I know she'll come around eventually," Elaine added at one point.

The following morning Dave left for his flight home. He realized that his visit had been a mistake long before he bid Debby a tearful good-bye at the airport.

Back in the Bitterroot Mountains, Dave waited and hoped for a summer visit when school was out, but such was not to be. He tried to arrange one in the summer of '74 when Debby was nine, but was told that it was not convenient. He could not argue with the child's guardians. It was close to Debby's birthday in '75 when the phone rang one evening. Dave answered.

"Hi, Dave, Rudy Gilmore here."

"Hi, Rudy. How's it going with you folks?"

"Not good, Dave...Debby's just completely out of hand. She's a darn good kid, but is absolutely obsessed with the thought that she has to return to you and the ranch. It's getting to be a daily battle. She ran away two weeks ago. Hitchhiking down the interstate. A trucker picked her up and dropped her off at the first weigh station he came to. She's doing terrible in school. But, Dave, her behavior is above board. She's really a good child."

"So how can I help?" Dave asked.

"Take her back."

Dave swallowed hard, his mind whirling like a sidewinder tornado.

"Dave?"

"Yeah, yeah, I'm still here...You want me to take her back?"

"Will you? We'll give you complete written authorization and all the other help we can, but Elaine and I just can't take any more of this constant bickering."

"OK, Rudy. When and how?"

"I'll put her on a plane in the morning and ship her clothes and things in a day or two."

"I'll meet the plane and we'll go from there. Call me when you have the flight information."

The phone went dead a second later.

Debby cried when they met at the airport. She was obviously glad to be back home. She started in her new fourth grade class with great enthusiasm. When school let out for the holidays in 1975, she brought home a report card with all As and Bs. Dave was dumbfounded.

Debby hit it off great with Joanne and Ed. The couple had no children of their own and Debby's arrival on the scene seemed to put a spark into their lives that wasn't there before. Debby spent lots of her free time with the Edwards down the road and talked weekly with her grandparents back in Fargo. It seemed as though she had never had any disagreement with them at all. She never discussed her motives or tried to alibi her early school problems. Debby simply tried her best to let bygones be bygones. She apologized to Elaine saying, "I know you all meant well, but I just needed to go home." In 1978 Rudy Gilmore died. Dave and Debby went to Fargo and attended the funeral.

In 1981, when Glenn Edwards passed away, Debby was seventeen. She took Glenn's death quite hard. Beth stayed on the small ranch for almost a year as she liquidated her assets. Then she moved to Eastern Montana where she had relatives. Dave bought the small ranch from her using the resources that he had amassed during his military career and the twelve years that he had been in Montana. He gave the house to Ed and Joanne as a major part of their ongoing salaries.

In 1982, Elaine Gilmore attended Debby's graduation at Darby High. Debby was the class president and graduated with a 3.94 grade average. That fall she entered the Montana State University in Bozeman. Elaine and Dave shared her college tuition costs equally.

In the beginning, Debby was home on the ranch for every vacation and spent her entire summers there with Dave, but time flew by. Late in her freshman year, disregarding everyone's advice, she married a young business major, and they soon had a child. The baby girl was named Margaret after Debby's mom. Debby received her BS degree in 1987, and the small family moved south to Fort Collins, Colorado, where Debby had been accepted for enrolment in Colorado State University's Veterinary College.

Dave hammered his way through life, loving every challenging aspect of his existence. Ed Petron had quietly slipped into the background as far as giving any orders or making veiled suggestions. After seventeen years, Dave realized that he was the true manager, the ramrod, of the Double Bar M. Ed and Joanne still were the ranch's primary source of manpower. Ed was milking the cow twice daily and collecting the eggs. He took what Dave didn't need back home, and Joanne sold the excess to several people in the area. Dave went to Ed one day in late June.

"Can you run the place for a few days?" he asked.

"Sure, Dave. No problem. Where you headed?"

"Debby's graduating down in Fort Collins. I'm going down to join in the festivities."

"Great! You give that gal my regards."

* * *

Dave boarded the plane, stowed his travel bag and his wide-brimmed Stetson in the overhead compartment, and settled down in his seat. It was just after daylight, and a hot day was in the making already. These conditions were not unusual for late June in western Montana. Inside the plane, the air-conditioner had maintained a comfortably cool environment. Dave was wearing casual Western clothes, jeans, shirt, and riding boots. Nothing fancy, just comfortable travel clothes. The open collar of his shirt showed a sunburned neck matching the rugged contour of his face. There was a babbling discord of voices as other passengers boarded and claimed their seats.

The stewardess stopped by Dave's row and started to usher a pleasant-looking business-type woman into the vacant window seat beside him. She paused as she placed her two small bags into the luggage compartment.

The woman leaned down to Dave. "Would you mind very much changing seats with me?"

"No problem," Dave replied, and moved over next to the window.

Dropping into her seat the woman immediately fastened her seat belt cinching it up tightly across her hips. From her handbag, she withdrew an open package of Ritz Crackers and nervously began nibbling on one.

The woman turned to Dave. "Thanks, I'm Judy Davenport... Have one?" she asked holding the package toward Dave.

"No thanks," he replied. "I'm Dave Logan...Pretty hot out there, isn't it," Dave noted.

"Nice in here. Where you headed?" the woman asked. She brushed cracker crumbs from the front of her light blue jacket and slacks.

"Cheyenne," Dave replied.

"Me too."

"Business trip?"

"No...I'm really headed for Fort Collins, but I have to change in Denver and Cheyenne. I work in Fort Collins, at the university."

"Oh. That's my destination eventually. What department do you work in?"

"At the library. I'm assistant librarian there."

"You ever meet a Deborah McCoskie by any chance?"

"Name doesn't ring a bell."

"She's my daughter. Vet school student."

"No. I'm afraid not. There are just too many kids to really remember any one of them."

"She graduates tomorrow," Dave proudly announced.

"Full degree?"

"DVM."

"Great. You must be really proud of her. That's a long haul for a young woman."

"Oh, I am."

The door of the plane thudded shut, and Dave felt the air pressure build slightly as the cabin was pressurized. He swallowed hard, clearing his ears. The pilot welcomed his passengers, cautioned everyone to buckle up, and the plane began its slow roll down the taxiway. They paused, awaiting takeoff clearance, and then the four big jets began to scream. The g-forces pressed Dave back into his seat, and he smiled. He loved that feeling of full thrust being applied. Suddenly the vibrations of being earthbound faded away, the nose of the aircraft pointed to the bright blue skies, and the plane hurtled seemingly straight up toward its cruising altitude. Everything was almost back to normal as the plane banked hard away from the looming mountains. In minutes, it picked up its proper heading for their southward journey and leveled off. Dave remembered vividly every action that the pilot and his crew were taking in these hectic moments of takeoff. He had sat at the controls of similar planes many times himself during his twenty-year career with the Air force.

"We made it," his seatmate muttered as she opened her eyes, unclasped her nervous hands, and flexed her fingers.

"Thought we might," Dave replied with a big grin.

They didn't talk much after that as the woman pulled a prizewinning novel from her purse and began to read. This gave Dave plenty of time to reflect on the past years leading up to today.

As his companion had said, "it had been a long haul." Debby had worked hard and had been an honor student all the way through. The day after tomorrow she would graduate with her long-sought-after degree.

"Is your wife coming to the graduation?" the woman suddenly asked.

"Afraid not, she died many years ago. It's been just Debby and me since she was five."

"Oh, I'm sorry. When we get in do you have a ride into Fort Collins? I have my car," the woman offered.

"Thanks anyway, but the family's meeting me."

The big airliner screeched in over the mile-high city of Denver and landed right on schedule. Dave's companion seemed not to be bothered by the landing at all.

"It's just those darn takeoffs that get to me," she explained with a wry grin.

They had a little over a two-hour wait for their connecting flight to Cheyenne, and Fort Collins. Dave and his traveling companion spent most of that interval at the busy coffee shop having a late breakfast together.

It was a quick and scenic thirty-five-minute flight up to Cheyenne and then a short hop down to Fort Collins. They climbed from the plane, and the woman turned and shook hands with Dave as they parted.

"Have a good time in Fort Collins," she suggested.

"I'm sure I will," he answered.

They parted and Dave headed for the baggage reclaim area. The woman turned toward the street carrying her two small bags.

"Grandpa!" a voice shouted, and Dave swung about. Out of the small crowd darted a blond, blue-eyed whirlwind. She ran toward the man with arms outstretched. The child wore tennis shoes, blue jeans, and a Denver Bronco jersey. Dave dropped to one knee and caught her in a quick embrace.

"Hi there, Peggy," he greeted. "You look pretty as ever."

"I'm glad you could come," the child replied. "I miss you so much." Dave rose to his feet.

"Hi, Dave," another voice began. "It's so good to see you again."

Dave turned and took his daughter in his arms. He kissed her cheek and gave her a warm hug. He leaned down slightly and whispered in her ear, "Hi, Spider." He released his hold on her with his right arm and gripped the hand of the young man standing beside her. "Hi, Jim. Haven't seen you in a couple of years."

"At least that long. But all that's about to become a thing of the past."

"I hope so," Dave replied.

"Where's your suitcase?" little Peggy asked.

"Right there, the big black bag." Dave pointed to the heavy piece that had just been brought in from the plane. "But it's too much for you." Dave handed his small overnight case to the little six-year-old.

"I've got it, Dave," the younger man offered as he retrieved the big piece of luggage.

They headed out of the terminal a moment later. Dave walked beside his daughter with one arm about her strong shoulders.

Debby McCoskie had the looks and poise of a professional. She was sure of herself, strong, capable, and ready to take on the world at large. She wore shabby high-heeled riding boots, faded jeans, and a Western-style cotton shirt that accented her rich figure to just the right degree. A long blond ponytail was threaded through the hole above the adjusting band in the back of her baseball cap. Tiny turquoise earrings in the shape of small dogs dangled from her ear lobes. Dave could tell that she wore no makeup. In fact, just like her mother, she needed none. Her complexion was dark and natural, having submitted to the effects of the elements during the many years of her outdoor existence. She wore rimless glasses with a faint rose tint in the upper sections of the lenses.

The man walking ahead of them was taller than Dave by an inch or so, but not as heavy. He was athletic looking, strong, and capable. He wore an expensive Stetson, a plaid long-sleeved Western shirt, and blue jeans. His shirt was held together at the throat by a bolo tie with a bright sterling silver and turquoise clasp, and his riding boots had been buffed recently to a brilliant shine. The man had a ruddy Western complexion and sported a neatly trimmed full dark beard.

He led the way to the family's Ford Bronco and, unlocking the doors, placed the big piece of luggage in the back. Little Peggy tossed the other case in with it. They all climbed in and began the short eight-mile trip down to Fort Collins. Dave rode in the front seat with his son-in-law. He sat almost sideways so that he could look at and converse with his daughter. Little Peggy rode in the backseat with her mom.

"We've got you a good motel room right off campus just like you wanted," Deborah advised.

"Sounds good to me. I won't be here that long anyway."

"When you going back?" asked Jim.

"Day after tomorrow. Got work to do."

"Typical rancher, aren't you?" Deborah replied.

"How's the real estate business going, Jim?" Dave asked.

"Really good all spring, but it's slowed down a little right now. Still, I can't complain."

"When you all move north, have you got any plans, Jim, anything worked out for yourself up there in the valley?"

"No, Dave, nothing yet. Thought I'd just wait till I got up there and saw what was in store. Then I'll decide on what and where."

They were in Fort Collins shortly, and Jim took the scenic drive around the city and the campus before dropping Dave off at his motel. They would all meet for supper later that evening.

"Can I stay with Gramps?" little Peggy asked.

The gramps said "sure," but the other two adults in unison replied, "No." A short discussion ensued after which Dave and little Peggy stood on the curb and waved good-bye as the car turned away into the city's traffic.

In the motel, Peggy settled down to watch some cartoons on the television while Dave headed for the bathroom. He turned on the water in the shower and then stood by the sink looking at himself in the mirror. He grimaced in pain one time and from the pocket of his jeans retrieved a small bottle of pills. He shook one out into his hand, thought for a moment, added a second one, and downed these without water. Soaking a washcloth in cold water he held it firmly against the back of his head as he settled down to rest on the toilet seat. Dave sat there with his eyes closed, his aching head in his hands for several minutes.

He could feel the medication taking effect already. This attack had come on very quickly, only a few minutes ago, and he knew that he would shake it off just as fast. Down the road, it would be a much different story. Already the seizures were more frequent and more severe, and during their onslaught, his vision often became blurred.

His doctors had predicted all of these signs several months ago. Early on, they had thought that the deep-seated brain tumor was slow in its growth, but at his last visit they found it had almost doubled in size. The die had been cast. From the very beginning, the medicos had wanted surgery and a ritual of chemotherapy, radiation, the whole works, to maybe give him a few more months. They weren't talking years; they were hoping to extend his life only for a few more months. Dave had refused all of their suggestions, opting to simply try to control the painful spasms, and other outward signs, as long as he could. He had too much on his mind, too much to do, in the short period of life that remained for him. For most of his remaining days, he couldn't afford to be wasting time, sitting in waiting rooms, undergoing treatments in the care of the AMA. He hoped no one would know of his decision, or find out.

He felt better a few minutes later, turned off the running water in the shower, and rejoined his granddaughter in the room. The child turned off the TV, looked at her idol, and asked about the ranch.

"Can I have my own dog, Gramps?" she asked. "Mom said I'd have to ask you."

"I've got one now that you can play with, but just maybe I can find you one of your own. We'll see."

Later that evening they all gathered and ate great steak dinners at a famous local restaurant. At one point in the meal Dave looked across at Deborah and asked, "You all driving up when you come?"

"Yes. We'll rent a small U-Haul van to carry all our stuff. We haven't got much. Our apartment's furnished. Jim will drive the van, and I'll drive the Bronco."

"I'll be looking for you every day. When do you think you'll be leaving here?" Dave asked.

"Two or three days," Jim offered. "Yesterday was my last day at the agency. After tomorrow all we have to do is finish packing, load up, and take off."

"It'll be so wonderful to be really going home for good," Deborah said. "To be back with the open land, the mountains, the cattle, and all the animals. That's what it's all about. All of those visits were great over the years, but there's nothing like knowing that you're going home to stay. You know, Dave? It's been over eight years since I really lived there on the bench with you."

"I know exactly what you mean. I've missed you too. I moved most of my stuff to the bunkhouse the other day. The house will be all ready for you guys when ever you get there."

Jim and Deborah looked quickly at each other, and then Deborah asked, "You did what?"

"I'm moving to the bunkhouse. There's only two bedrooms in the house, you know that."

"I know, but we're planning to add another bedroom and bath on the back side, right next to where the office is. Jim and I will use my old room and Peggy can sleep on the couch for a few weeks till we get the addition completed."

"Nuts. You guys take the house. I'll be just fine out there. Remember I started out living in that bunkhouse, and it suited me just fine." Dave smiled as he remembered.

"I recall those days too," Deborah replied. "I remember helping you make the bed one time."

"That was the first night that I was there," Dave recalled.

"OK, but when we get the extra rooms built you'll move back to the house?" Jim stated.

"We'll see how everything goes."

They completed their meal and dropped Dave off at his motel. Tomorrow would be a busy and exciting day for all of them, so they all turned in early, resting up for what was to be.

Dave was up before the sun the following day as was his habit. He ate a quick breakfast, at a small eatery adjacent to the motel, and then headed by cab for the university's commencement activities scheduled for 10:00 a.m. He met Jim and Peggy outside the hall, and they found seats together in the family section of the audience. The ceremonies were short and sweet with the commencement address being given by the dean of the institution. The procession of graduates followed, and Dave felt tears brewing in his eyes as Deborah McCoskie's name was announced, and the young woman stepped up to receive her diploma and vestments. Her decorative hood and the edges of her robe were done in gray velvet. Soon the formalities were over, and the graduates and the guests all mingled for an hour of greetings and refreshments.

Dave located Deborah and, taking the young woman in his arms, gave her a well-deserved hug in reward of her accomplishment. With her fingers, little Peggy traced the smooth velvet trimmings of her mother's gown. Dave took Deborah aside, away from the crowd. He held her at arm's length for a quiet moment.

The man's eyes brimmed with tears for an instant as he looked into Deborah's eyes. "Your mom was here today, Spider. I could feel her right by my side. It was uncanny. I know she was there, and she was so proud of you." A tear escaped and ran unchecked down Dave's cheek.

Deborah reached up with the edge of her gown's sleeve and wiped the wetness away.

"You loved Mom very much didn't you, Dave?" she asked.

Dave only nodded as he struggled to regain his control. They turned back toward the others. Deborah slipped out of her gown and folded it across her arm. Beneath the robe, she was wearing a lightweight, summer dress. She was beautiful and Dave felt another big burst of sentimental pride as he looked at her.

THE BEST LAID PLANS OF MICE AND MEN...

"You know, Dave? I owe all of this to you," Deborah reminded him, holding up her rolled diploma for emphasis. "You're the one who encouraged me and put me through all those years of schooling. It must not have been easy."

"It wasn't only me," Dave admitted. "The proceeds from your ranch kept us all going...And your grandparents had set aside money too." Dave added.

"But you ran the ranch. You still made it all possible."

Dave couldn't argue the point successfully. He quietly muttered, "I enjoyed every minute of it," and let the subject evaporate. They finished out the day with a gala dinner at one of the area's best restaurants and then parted for a welcomed night's sleep.

The following day the family drove Dave back to the airport. Here he caught his northbound flight heading for Montana and a much less complicated way of life. As the plane lifted off, Dave heaved a sigh of relief. Deep down, he detested civilization and all its wild hubbub of activity. Life was too short for everyone to be in such a big hurry, racing madly it seemed to reach an uncertain end.

Below the plane's wings, the landscape became almost devoid of cities, towns, and houses. Soon it was wooded mountain slopes and scattered fields. In late afternoon, they slipped into Missoula's airport. Dave retrieved his luggage and climbed into his pickup. He headed south down the long highway. He would cover the seventy-some miles to the ranch well before bedtime.

* * *

Dave turned off the paved West Fork Road and stopped to check the mailbox fastened atop a heavy post. The box was empty. "*Ed must have picked up the mail earlier,*" he muttered to himself. He drove up the narrow gravel roadway between the spacious hay fields. They looked good, almost ready to cut. Just before he started to climb, he passed between the old barn complex and, on the other side of the road, the small, modern, single-story, home. Dave had bought the old Edwards' spread back in '81 and, unbeknownst to Deborah, had placed the small ranch on the books in her name. Ed and Joanne lived there rent-free as a major part of their salary. Dave beeped his horn twice as he drove past, signaling that he was home.

A few minutes later, he topped out on the bench, as the locals called the area, and in the fading light noted the flashing streams of the irrigation sprinklers as they clicked on through the night, watering his upper hay fields. As he pulled to a stop by the bunkhouse his Australian sheep dog, Andy, came racing to meet him, barking happily as he came.

"Down, Andy!" Dave snapped, and the dog immediately dropped to his haunches. Dave ruffled his fur, scratched his ears and chest, and then released him with a curt, "OK!—You be good now."

He gathered up his luggage and, entering the small bunkhouse, dropped the two pieces on the bed. He closed the door and walked to the main house pausing to listen to the constant clatter of the many irrigation heads as they clicked rhythmically in the waning rays of the setting sun. He walked into the kitchen through the unlocked back door and from the refrigerator retrieved a can of beer.

Dave turned on the light momentarily in the small office and glanced at the mail and the note pads lying there on his desk. He found nothing of great importance. He stepped out into the quiet yard and settled down in a very dilapidated lawn chair that just barely tolerated his weight. From where he sat, it looked like his garden was doing all right, although he knew it probably could stand some weeding. His primary thoughts were of his cattle, currently north of the ranch proper on Forest Service grazing land. He would ride out tomorrow and check on them. He knew Ed and Joanne would handle the irrigation chores and the other livestock just as they always did.

The following morning Dave fixed and ate his breakfast before the sun managed to struggle above the Sapphire Mountains. He heard Ed's pickup arrive and on the way to the corral, Dave stopped by the milking parlor. He found the man just finishing milking the family milk cow. Joanne would bottle and deliver several quarts of the rich milk to other neighbors sometime during the day.

"How was the trip, Dave?" the man asked as he chased the little Jersey cow out of the barn.

THE BEST LAID PLANS OF MICE AND MEN...

"Good."

"Deborah graduated all right, I imagine."

"Sure. It was great. They'll be coming up here in a few days. Probably within the week. I'm going out to look at the cattle this morning. What you got planned?"

"Change the pipes. Joanne's going to shift the flood set down on the lower two fields. I'll probably pull the cutter blades out of the two mowing machines. Need to have them sharpened before haying time comes along."

"Talk to you later," Dave said as he turned away and headed for the corral.

It was a little cooler once he rode into the trees covering the rolling foothills below Dakota Peak. Andy ranged ahead of the horse and rider sniffing every hummock and tuft of grass that he came upon. He instinctively raised a hind leg and watered many of these. Dave rode for almost an hour before he spotted his herd. They were everywhere browsing through the trees. By close to noon he figured that he had located most of the four hundred head of stock, and they all looked well. Of the four hundred about two hundred were big beef cows. Several great bulls ranged here and there among the herd and nearly two hundred head of big fat calves wandered about through the trees with their mothers.

On his way back to the ranch, he swung just a little to the west and approached a shallow dry wash cutting abruptly down the slope through the trees. He followed it for a short distance and then found where the terrain opened up into an area containing less brush and foliage. He reined up and sat his horse for several long minutes. Before leaving the corral, he somehow knew that he would swing by this place today.

This dry wash was where Peg Martin, Deborah's mother, had died. She had been Dave's wife for less than a month.

Dave passed up lunch, as he often did on these hot summer days, and after caring for his horse went to work moving his remaining personal items from the house. By supper time, he was comfortably settled in the bunkhouse and had given the master bedroom a thorough cleaning. Deborah's old room was already spic-and-span. Dave figured that he'd clean the rest of the house later. It wasn't in too bad shape regardless. His twenty years in the military had prepared him well to assume the roll of housekeeper.

A week had passed and every day he expected to hear word or see the family arriving. Still there was nothing. He was beginning to worry slightly. He was down in the lower hay fields one afternoon with Joanne Bailey shifting a flood irrigation dam. Dave wore his knee-length rubber boots, but Joanne was content just wading around thigh deep with just a pair of old jogging shoes on her feet. Her jeans were soaked, but she didn't care. The thirty-six-year-old woman, born and bred in a ranching family, was good at her job. Her companion, Ed, was fourteen years her senior, but this didn't seem to matter to either of them. She wielded a shovel better than many men would have under the circumstances, and Dave was working up a sweat trying to keep up with her. His saddle horse grazed quietly along the perimeter of the field, and Andy lay curled up in the shade, paying little attention to anything going on. They finished their set and Joanne turned to head back for her house a short distance down the slope beyond the trees.

"Good job, Joanne," Dave said as he shouldered his shovel and headed across the field toward his horse.

"Don't mind this kind of work on hot days like today," the young woman replied. "It's nice and cool wading around in the ditch. I've got to go get Ed's supper going."

Dave laughed. "I know what you mean. I'll see you tomorrow."

* * *

They parted and Dave had almost reached his horse when he heard the traffic coming up the road. Through the screening timber, Dave caught a glimpse of a bright red Ford Bronco. A moment later, through the thin dust cloud, he spotted the brilliant markings of a U-Haul van. He swung aboard his mount and forded the small creek that ran just below the road. Carrying his shovel like a cavalry guidon, he headed for the house. As Dave moved up the road, Andy heard the strangers and immediately took off at a dead run for the house.

Dave whistled shrilly once and yelled, "Andy!" The animal stopped in his tracks.

"It's all right, Andy. Be good."

The dog seemed to nod his head in agreement, turned again, and raced up the road for home. Just as the barn came in sight, Dave heard the dog barking excitedly. He trotted up over the final rise and saw the family. Peggy and Andy were running together with the child waving a stick that the dog was trying to snatch from her hand. The little girl spotted Dave coming, stopped quickly, and hurled the piece of wood as far as she could. She changed course and raced in her grandfather's direction. Dave pulled his big gelding to a halt, swung from the saddle, and stood his shovel up against the bulk fuel tank next to the driveway. Ground-reining his horse, he stooped down to grab the happy child in his arms.

"Hi, Peggy." He smiled as he hoisted the child into the saddle.

Peggy laughed happily as Dave picked up his reins and walked the short distance to the parked vehicles. When he arrived, he lifted the little girl down and turned to the waiting adults.

"Have a good trip, Jim?" Dave asked, gripping the other's extended hand.

"No problems at all."

"Welcome home, Spider," he greeted and, stepping close to Deborah, gave her a big hug.

"It's so good to be home...Finally, at long last, I'm really home." Deborah hugged Dave for long moments as she turned her head round and round scrutinizing the scene. "It's always the same, just like I remember from day one. Nothing ever changes."

"Didn't need to change anything. Your dad and mom had it all just right when I came along. All I do is try and keep it the way they left it."

"Yes. You painted the house...What was it, last year?"

"Year before actually. All the corral rails were replaced this past winter. A few things like that, but really nothing's changed. Come see the house."

"Wolf isn't here anymore," Deborah remembered.

"I know...He was a great dog."

"Remember how he never, ever, barked?"

"Probably the wolf in him," Dave replied.

Dave led the way to the old familiar structure, opened the screen door, and held it back for the threesome to enter. He kicked off his knee-high rubber boots and pulled on his battered riding boots that stood just inside the door. Deborah glanced at the small kitchen, and then moved directly to the master bedroom. She paused at the doorway taking in every detail of the neat, clean, and orderly room. It was obviously a room awaiting new occupants with fresh towels and washcloths lying neatly on the foot of the bed.

"You've moved out, Dave," she said.

"Couple of days ago. I'm quite comfortable where I am."

"Oh, Dave," she muttered as she shook her head sadly. Deborah hugged him briefly before she turned and walked slowly through the rest of the house. At the door to her old bedroom, she paused. "This is your room now, Peggy. I want you to keep it nice and clean just like Gramps fixed it for you." The child ducked past the adults and threw herself across the bed.

"I will," she promised.

"Can I back the van up to the house across the grass without hurting it?" Jim asked.

"Sure. It's dry and hard. Won't hurt a thing," Dave advised. "I'll help you unload after I put my horse up."

"Just take it easy, Dave. You've been hard at it all day. I can unload the few things that we need right off."

Dave agreed and a minute later gathered up the reins of his horse. With Peggy close by his side, he headed for the corral. He unsaddled the horse and rubbed it down for several minutes. Peggy sat on the upper rail of the corral watching intently as her grandfather worked. Glancing at her from the corner of his eye, Dave saw the child's mother, over twenty years ago, sitting in the same position. The chore was at last finished, and Dave slipped the bridle from the mount's head, gave him a slap on the rump, and watched as the animal dashed out into the middle of the big corral. He immediately rubbed his nose and forelegs together. Then he threw himself down into the dirt, rolled completely onto his back, and then squirmed back and forth rubbing dirt into his freshly groomed coat. He lurched to his feet, spread all four legs wide apart, and shook violently, sending a cloud of dust into the air. Done with all of that, he trotted over to the tiny creek that ran through one corner of the corral and drank.

"Come on, Peggy. We've got to go get supper started," the man advised, as he reached up to help the child down.

As Dave and Peggy walked up the driveway past the big garden area, Jim drove the small van off the lawn and parked it beside Dave's pickup. They found Deborah busy in the kitchen thawing out a package of hamburger in a skillet on the stove.

"I've already got one thawed out," Dave said opening the refrigerator door and placing the other package on the counter.

"I saw that," the woman remarked. "And the chopped up onion and green pepper. I take it we're having spaghetti tonight?"

"That was the idea," Dave replied.

"The problem is there're four of us tonight, not just you." Deborah laughed happily and, turning Dave around, gave him a gentle shove toward the living room.

"I can fix it," he complained.

"Not around here! Not anymore, you won't. You stay the hell out of my kitchen."

Dave froze for an instant. Deborah's mother had said the exact same thing to him twenty-two years ago in this very same room. Standing there, Deborah looked very much like her mother. There was a startling resemblance, and one could easily see the mother/daughter relationship. The only major difference that Dave could see was the fact that Deborah had blond hair, while her mother's hair had been a dark auburn shade.

Deborah's spaghetti was OK, but not quite as good as what Dave could have produced himself. At the conclusion of the meal, the woman turned to Dave and asked, "You have anything for dessert?"

"Sure do," he replied and, slipping out of his seat, turned to the small pantry just off the kitchen, next to the bathroom. "Here we go," he announced and placed a large apple pie on the table. It was very obviously homemade. He turned to a cabinet and produced four small plates and from a drawer under the counter a pastry spatula.

"You bake that?" Deborah asked, frowning as Dave began slicing the pie.

"No. Not me. A friend of mine baked it. She knew you were coming."

"Anyone I might know?"

"Betty Johnson. Remember her?"

"No. I'm afraid not."

"Her husband was one of the local farriers. Used to shoe all your dad's and mom's horses. Eric died back in '85. Remember?"

"Oh yes. Seems like I do remember him…What's she doing now?"

"Running a little restaurant down in Darby. Good place to eat, but nothing fancy."

"You see her often?"

"Just on Saturday nights usually. We hit the town, have a couple of suds, and dance for a bit."

"I'll have to go by and thank her for this," Deborah exclaimed. "It's great!"

The kitchen chores were done shortly and the three adults settled down for a short time in the living room. Darkness was dropping slowly across the bench and Dave rose from the couch and headed for the door.

"I'm going to bed. See you guys in the morning."

"The house is always open, Dave," Jim promised.

"Yes. I know, thanks."

In the bunkhouse Dave flopped down on the bed fully clothed, listening to the rattling chorus of the sprinklers as they pulsed endlessly throughout the night. A cool breeze from the mountains drifted through the open window, bringing with it the sweet smell of growing grass and the occasional whiff of cattle and horses.

He finally rose and undressed. As he rested, images of his wife and Deborah as a child flashed across his mind. It was a blessing, he knew, to have such fond memories. Minutes later, he was asleep.

* * *

Lights were already on in the house when Dave crossed the yard the following morning. Deborah had breakfast almost ready and thrust a steaming cup of coffee into his hand as he settled down at the side of the table.

"Your place is at the head, Dave," Deborah stated.

"No! That's your spot, or Jim's."

THE BEST LAID PLANS OF MICE AND MEN...

"Dave?" the woman began, but then froze, speechless, doubting that she could win this argument.

"If it's going to be a problem, maybe we should just get a round table," Dave quietly suggested with a grin.

"Oh, all right, Dave," she relented hotly. "Sit where ever you want."

Jim and Peggy joined them, and they all ate a hearty breakfast. Following the meal Dave took Jim and the child for a tour of the ranch buildings, pointing out all the hazards, all the dangers, and explaining all of the dos and don'ts, especially for the child's benefit. Other times over the years, he had done the same thing when they had visited before, but he always felt better with a refresher course under his belt. Returning to the house, he found Deborah just finishing her morning chores.

"I'm going to town," Jim said. "Thought I'd check out the real estate markets in the area and see what's available. I'll unload the rest of our things when I get back. Later on, I'll chop out some weeds in your garden, Dave, if you don't mind. That's about all I know how to do around here right now."

"Sounds good," Dave began. "I'm sitting down with Deborah to go over the books for a while and then I'm taking her to town myself. We should be back by lunchtime."

"Can I go with Daddy?" Peggy asked.

Both parents agreed. Dave ushered Deborah into the small office and seated her in the battered swivel chair at the desk. He placed sheet after sheet of financial documents before her. She scrutinized the pages one by one feeling uneasy, more and more overwhelmed, as the minutes ticked by.

"How can this be, Dave?" she asked puzzled. "I had no idea..." The woman thumbed through the sheets again, punching data into a calculator on the desk top as she went. At last, she pushed the final sheet aside and hit the total key. Deborah literally fell back in her chair and raised her questioning eyes to meet Dave's.

"That's your bottom line, Spider. That's what you've got to work with from here on out," Dave advised.

"But how did you manage this?" she asked gesturing toward the calculator.

"Remember, I have my military retirement coming in every month, and I had a small salary every year too that your grandparents forced on me years ago. I never needed any of the proceeds from your ranch. I banked it all every year for you."

"But the expenses?"

"They all came out of your income," Dave replied. "It's all in the ledgers, plus and minus."

"My schooling for eight years and all those costs?"

"Your grandparents, you remember the Gilmores? They paid about half, and I chipped in for the rest," Dave stated.

"I remember Grandma Elaine, but Grandpa Rudy died when I was very young. I thought my schooling was coming out of the ranch income."

"Nope. I managed to hang onto all of that for you as best I could. Remember this though…It's been a great twenty years in the cattle business. This market undoubtedly won't last forever. But there's your bottom line, Spider. There's your nest egg." Dave reached down and indicated the bright green numbers staring at them from the face of the calculator. In his heart, he was very proud.

There was a long minute of utter silence in the small room. Deborah finally reached out and switched the calculator off, bundled the sheets of financial records neatly together, and slipped them into the top drawer of the desk. She rose from her seat and for a long speechless minute stared almost blankly at her stepfather. Then she smiled and threw her arms around his neck. She kissed him several times as tears rolled quietly down her cheeks.

"Let's go to town, Spider," Dave finally suggested. "I want to show you something."

Deborah pushed herself away. "Give me a couple of minutes," she replied as she left the office and turned toward the bathroom.

Dave climbed into his big mud-streaked Dodge pickup. The truck had no tailgate, and Andy took a flying leap and settled down in the truck bed where he loved to ride. Deborah came from the house a minute later and climbed into the cab beside her stepfather.

They headed down the gravel road and as they passed Ed Petron's place the woman turned to Dave and said, "I remember quite clearly spending time down here with Beth and Glenn Edwards. They were the most fun."

"Yes, they were great people. Helped your mom and dad often. Helped me a lot right after your mom died."

"You bought their place, didn't you, after Glenn passed away?"

"Yes, but it'll really be yours someday."

"What do you mean by that?" Deborah asked.

"I bought it in my name with my savings, but it goes to you and yours when I'm gone. It'll all be part of the Double Bar M someday."

"You bought it with your savings?"

"Well yes. I had a pile of dough that I saved while in the Air Force. I was going to buy my own place somewhere if I enjoyed ranching. I found that I did like this way of life and figured that I'd just stay where I was. I owed you and your mother that much. You'd given me a chance and an open-ended contract, so to speak. Remember?"

"Yes, Dave, but gee whiz. That was your money."

"So what. Call it a graduation present or something. Anyway, the land's yours down the road. After all, who else have I got to leave it to?"

"You're so damned sentimental," the woman muttered.

A few minutes later, they moved slowly down Main Street of the small town. They swung past the high school complex, made a U-turn, and headed south again.

"Hasn't changed much here, has it?" Deborah noticed. They retraced their path down the several blocks of the center of town again. "There's Jim's car," she suddenly exclaimed, pointing to the empty vehicle.

Dave drove on, and right at the town's city limits sign, pulled off on the soft shoulder. Directly across the highway was an old service station. It seemed deserted and the huge *For Sale* sign seemed to be telling them why.

"There you go, Spider," Dave said pointing to the property.

"What?" she asked.

"You said that you wanted to open your own vet clinic and office. Well here's just what you want. It's inside the town limits, five acres, city water, no zoning restrictions, and really anxious sellers holding their hands out and simply begging for an offer."

"But, Dave. It's a damned gas station."

"A bulldozer will level all those buildings in half a day. They're not worth much anyway. You saw the books awhile ago. You've got the money to invest. The closest vet around here is almost thirty miles up the valley. If you don't want to spend ranch funds for the place, I'll lend you what you need. I still have a little left."

"My God, you're crazy as a loon," Deborah muttered. "The big problem is, you're serious!" she replied.

"Absolutely. You can live at the ranch. After all it's your home, and it's only a few minutes from here. Peggy will have the same great environment to grow up in that you had, and I know Jim will find something here in the valley that appeals to him." There was a long period of silence while Deborah thought. At last Dave turned to her again. "Spider?"

"Yes. I'm thinking…Let's just go home right now. This is all happening too fast. I've got to talk this over with Jim too. We've managed to save up a little bit over the years to get my business started with. And we wanted to add a room to the house. I'll just have to think and put it all together piece by piece. After all, Dave, we have priorities."

Dave nodded his agreement and pulled back onto the highway heading for home. They were almost there when Deborah turned to him with a question.

"Do you know any reputable architects and contractors that we could talk with?"

"None personally, but I'll do some checking for you."

"Thanks, Dave," she answered as they pulled into the ranch yard.

* * *

After supper that night, Dave and Jim walked slowly down the road. As they did, Dave explained the basics of their two irrigation systems, flood and sprinkler, and told him all about the main ditch system that fed the ranch from high up in the foothills.

"You been on a horse much?" Dave asked.

"Once or twice is all. I wouldn't consider myself as being experienced at all."

"If you've got time, I'll put you on one tomorrow, and give you a real tour of the place. How'd it go in town today? Anything sound interesting?"

"One small company, a one-man show really, is interested in me. Bert Mason Realty. You know him?"

"Met him once or twice. Seems like an all right guy."

"After what I'm used to, down in the Colorado areas north of Denver, this town is dead. I'd be lucky if I could come up with one sale a month around here. With Bert's offer I'd work every other week, and, as he said, 'go fishing the other week.'"

Dave laughed. "At least you'd be keeping in touch with the trends and all that. Consider this too, Jim. Your living expenses will be almost zilch and you'd have damned near no business overhead."

They reached a place where the trees between the road and the stands of hay were thinly scattered. Over on the uphill side of the field Dave spotted Joanne Bailey knee deep in the ditch, scraping and shoveling tiny channels for the water to run through onto the field below her.

Jim spotted the woman too. "Who's that?" he asked.

"Joanne Bailey. She's my hired hand's significant other. Really a very nice young woman. Works like hell to earn her keep."

"Oh yes, Deborah told me about them. They live in the place right down there that you bought, right?"

"That's right."

"Doesn't she have any rubber boots to wear?" Jim asked.

"Says it's a waste of time. Says she gets them full of water anyway."

Jim chuckled. "Deb told me about the ranch finances, Dave. I don't see how you managed. We've been saving all we could ever since I got out of school. Our first challenge is going to be building an addition to the house so we have enough space for everybody. We wanted enough to get Deb's vet clinic started somewhere too."

"Build your clinic first. Did Deborah tell you about the parcel that I found just outside of town?"

"Yes. It sounds interesting. I'll talk to Bert about the possibilities tomorrow."

There was a long period of silence. At last, Joanne shouldered her shovel and trudged off down the field heading home. The hay was over knee high as she moved along.

"We'll cut those fields in a couple of weeks," Dave observed.

"She always work this late?"

"Joanne sees a need and fills it, anytime, anywhere."

"You know, Dave? If I go to work for Bert, I'd have every other week off. I never did enjoy fishing much. How long would it take for you to teach me to be a cattleman, a farmer maybe, something that would keep me busy all the time right here at home?"

"Forever, Jim. I've been at it since 1970. I knew nothing, but Deborah's mother took me under her wing and started teaching me full time. I haven't stopped learning yet, and it's been twenty-two years. But I guess with about four months behind me, I had a fair grip on the basics."

"And you've done an outstanding job!"

"I hired Ed Petron. He's one of the best ranch hands in the area. He's a great asset. Even if I weren't on the scene, you and Deborah had better keep him on the payroll. He's a great ramrod, to say the least."

"You have any other help?" Jim asked as they turned and began to retrace their steps back up the hill.

"Don't forget Joanne, she goes with Ed. I've got two others just part time. Like during the haying season and the roundup mostly. Joe Lucas and Lonnie Espanso. Lonnie's Mexican and a good hand, but the feds may catch up with him someday and send him back home."

"Oh, a wetback?"

Dave just nodded. As they neared the top of the hill, they spotted Deborah and Peggy coming from the direction of the house. Andy ran with them retrieving the stick that was thrown for him to fetch.

"Will you teach me what I need to know?" Jim asked in a quiet voice.

"Glad to try. There's a lot you'll need to know. Deborah too. But she's got a big edge on you. She worked this place with me for many years after she came back to live with me. Right up till she left for college. It was almost every night after school and most of her weekends too. I won't even mention her summer vacations. She was good on a horse and a tractor too. I imagine she still remembers most of those days. She was a capable hand back then, and I know she'll be an able hand if someday you two choose to run this place yourselves."

"She's a vet first," Jim stated.

"That's true," Dave replied just as the two groups met.

"What's true?" Deborah asked overhearing the last.

"You're a good vet," Jim responded.

They walked together toward the house. "Ice cream, anyone?" Deborah asked.

Jim and his daughter said, "Yes," but Dave backed away from the offer.

"It's been a long day," he answered. "I'm just going to turn in early."

They all said their good nights. Dave closed the bunkhouse door and immediately pulled his pill bottle from his jeans and popped two of the tiny orbs into his mouth. He turned on the cold water in the sink and, leaning down, splashed handfuls of the refreshing liquid time and again across the back of his head and neck. A few minutes later, he flopped fully clothed across his bed, listening to the faint music of the irrigation system and the whispered voice of the cool mountain breeze as it swirled gently around the eaves of the building.

***

The following day Dave took Deborah and Peggy up to Hamilton where they met with an architect and a contractor. Very basic ideas were exchanged concerning the design and construction on the Darby property. While they were thus engaged, Jim was in meetings with the property owners and the realtors involved. They were all back at the house just before noon with many facts and figures to mull over in the following days.

They finished eating lunch and Peggy took off to play with Andy. Dave and the other adults lingered at the table with their coffee discussing many eventualities and possibilities. It would all be a wait-and-see issue as the parties involved contemplated the offer that Jim had made for the old service station. Deborah excused herself and went to the door to check on Peggy.

"Question, Dave?" Jim said.

"Shoot."

"The historical ownership of this property, the Double Bar M, can you spell that all out for me?" Jim asked. "Deb's told me some, but it's still a little confusing."

"Glad to...Deborah's great grandfather Hiram Martin is as far back as I have any knowledge." Dave reached back and grabbed a scratch pad and pencil from the counter and began to sketch a family tree as he explained. "Hiram died in a barn fire back in the early '30s. The ranch came down to his son, Richard. Richard ran the place until he and his wife died in an auto crash in '49. Their son Lou took over at that time. He had just recently married Deborah's mom. Deborah didn't come along until much later, up in '64. Peg's husband, Lou, died in March of 1970. Peg hired me in June of the same year. I married her in October, and she died only a few weeks later." Deborah returned to the table overhearing the end of Dave's explanation.

"Your dad willed the ranch to your mom?" Jim asked his wife.

"Yes," she replied, "and mom left it to me."

"Didn't Peg leave any share of the ranch to you, Dave, in her will?"

"No. It was completely in Deborah's name, 100 percent. Deborah was the only legal heir to the ranch. Remember, Montana's not a community property state. Even if Peg had changed her will after we were married, it would have done no good. She died too soon after the change was made, and the change would have been declared null and void."

"Well then, how did..."

Dave held up his hand. "How'd I get involved—"That's simple enough. I didn't! Legally I have never figured in this, at least I didn't before 1980. When Peg died, Deborah's grandparents, on her mother's side, were appointed as Deborah's legal guardians. Then in 1981, when Grandpa Rudy died, I petitioned the court and took over as Deborah's guardian. Grandma Elaine was all for it. Debby had lived at home the previous six years with me and was fifteen at the time. I became her guardian for a few years until she reached the age of accountability.

Today, ever since Debby turned twenty-one, I'm technically not in the picture at all. I'm Deborah's hired hand, her foreman, if you will. I draw wages the same as Ed and Joanne."

"Oh, Dave, that's not true," the woman exclaimed, with tears brimming in her eyes. "You're far more than that to me. You're the only father I've ever known." The woman rose from the table, crossed to Dave's side, and threw her arms about his shoulders.

"I know all that, Spider. I'm simply talking the legalities of it all. You're the greatest daughter any man could ever hope for." Dave reached back and circled Deborah's waist with his arm and returned her embrace. As the discussions concerning the legal positions on the ranch were completed, silence descended on the kitchen for many minutes. Dave finally pushed back his chair.

"Let's go for a ride, Jim," he suggested.

The two men spent the entire afternoon on horseback. They ended up high in the foothills where their main ditch began. Andy was their ever-present companion darting here and there in pursuit of some figment or other of his imagination. The concrete weir channeled water from Conise Creek and headed it downgrade toward the ranch. They had legal water rights to this water and it was a yearlong adequate supply. They followed the ditch back and, when they reached the uppermost hay field, spotted Ed Petron in the process of changing one of the long sets of sprinkler lines. They ground-reined their horses at the head of the line and walked out to meet him. Andy had had enough and he took off down the slope, headed for home. The wet hay was over knee high and, before they reached the center of the field, they were both soaking wet to above their knees.

Ed paused in his work as they approached. "Ed, I want you to meet Deborah's husband. Jim McCoskie. — Jim, this is the guy to rely on, he's the one with all the right answers, Ed Petron."

The two men shook hands and Ed laughed self-consciously at Dave's open compliments. Dave and Ed started right in with their first lesson concerning the downhill movement of a sprinkler irrigation line. Each of the forty-foot sections of three-inch pipe had a sprinkler head fastened to a two-foot-tall pipe at its far end. Each section had to be unhooked from the old line, carried downhill about forty feet and reconnected to the new line.

The lines were not heavy, but it was a balancing act to move them around. Water flowed constantly from the open end of the new line, and one had to work quickly to get the new pipe connected. With three of them working, the line was finished in just minutes. Jim caught on quickly. With a thud, Ed dropped the final section into place and the line blossomed into a massive fountain of pulsing sprinklers. Several had become clogged with chaff, and Dave showed Jim how to clean these heads out without getting drowned.

They rode their horses back to the ranch and unsaddled them while Ed turned to the milk cow standing patiently by the door to the milking parlor. He opened the door for her, and she obediently entered and stepped into the stanchion awaiting her ration of grain.

Dave and Jim headed for the house. Peggy saw them coming and jumped from her swing and came running. Deborah slammed the back door of the small U-Haul van and waited for the men to reach her.

"It's empty, Jim. You can turn it in anytime," she remarked.

"Should have waited, Deb. I'd have helped you with that stuff."

"No problem. By the way, call Bert Mason. He wants to speak to you."

They all went to the house. By now, the men's wet feet and jeans had dried enough that they posed no problem. Jim turned toward the office, and Dave grabbed a beer from the refrigerator. He settled down at the kitchen table, while Deborah started working on her evening meal.

"Need milk, Deborah? Ed asked as he entered the house.

The woman turned to the refrigerator, opened the door, and took inventory. "I could use one," she stated. "And have Joanne bottle me a full quart of good heavy cream if you will. I love whipped cream for making desserts."

The man placed a quart of milk on the counter. "Bring you the cream tomorrow?" he asked.

"That'll be fine. I'm in no hurry," Deborah agreed. Ed turned away, taking the remaining bottles of fresh milk with him, and headed home.

"They took our offer," Jim announced happily as he entered the kitchen. He dropped down in a chair beside Dave. "Bert talked with the bank too. The numbers look great all the way around. Like five percent fixed rate. It's right in line with our budget, just what we hoped for."

"You should buy it outright. Don't finance it!" Dave cautioned.

"It's better for us to let the bank carry the note," Jim stated. "It's a business, and the interest and other factors are all deductible. It'll work out better for us this way."

"Well, I guess you know what you're doing," Dave stated with a shrug.

"We've got the down payment ourselves. All we need is a loan from the ranch to pay for the buildings, equipment, and supplies."

"Loan, hell. There's enough in the ranch account for ten buildings. It's your money; for God's sake use it."

Deborah produced two more beers, popped their tops, and handed one to Jim. "Here's to the Darby Veterinary Clinic," she toasted, and they all touched cans and drank deeply.

* * *

The McCoskies were absent much of the time for the next few days. They were busy ironing out their real estate transactions, settling on building design plans, and other construction details. They held a yard sale and got rid of all the old equipment that remained at the old station. After that, the wreckers arrived. In one day the service station was no more. Still it took almost a week to clear the property of all the debris. Deborah usually found time to fix their meals and Jim spent several hours almost every day working with Dave on whatever chores there were.

Dave went to Hamilton one morning for a load of grain and a supply of baler twine. Jim was busy this week handling the real-estate office while Bert Mason went fishing. Deborah spent a couple of hours down at the construction site where the contractor was pouring foundation and floor slabs. She returned home in midmorning and worked with Ed as he checked each of their tractors and mounted the necessary equipment for the harvesting of their all-important crop of hay.

Dave pulled into the ranch yard, parked, and carried two bags of groceries to the house. He met Peggy as she scampered through the back door. "There's more to bring in, Peggy. In the front seat," Dave ordered. The little girl ran toward the truck passing her mother on the driveway.

"What'd you get, Dave?" Deborah asked as she peeked into one of the store bags.

He didn't get a chance to answer for a loud cry, almost a scream, came from the truck. Deborah wheeled quickly and started toward the vehicle, but Dave caught her arm and quietly smiled. Peggy turned from the open door of the truck to face them holding a squirming beagle puppy tightly in her arms.

"Oh, Gramps," she began. "Is she mine?"

"Yes. But she's a he."

"He's so tiny," Peggy observed.

"He'll grow up pretty quick," Deborah advised.

"I'll call him Tiny," the girl replied as she turned away from the house with the puppy trailing behind her on its short leash.

Andy arrived about this time, but the moment went off without a hitch. The older dog simply chose to ignore the other one's presence.

"There's puppy food in one of these bags. And I don't think he's housebroken yet," Dave warned as he turned again and headed for the house.

Irrigation water was taken off the fields one by one, and after a two-day drying period, they all dove into the hardest part of the ranch year. Joe Lucas and Lonnie Espanso came to work every morning and stayed until quitting time, often after dark. To start with, Joanne and Ed each drove tractors mounted with mowing blades cutting the hay. They followed each other round and round the field. The tip of Joanne's mowing blade overlapped just slightly the area that Ed's machine had just cut. Thus, with each pass, they felled a swath of hay nearly twenty feet wide.

After the hay had dried for a couple of days, Joanne stopped mowing with her tractor. She began towing a large side-delivery rake, raking the hay into long windrows for baling or stacking. Before the baling took place, the windrows were rolled over again with the big rake to complete the drying cycle.

Ed usually drove their biggest tractor, towing the John Deere hay baler. Joe and Lonnie followed him through the fields with the Jeep pulling the big flatbed trailer. They loaded and hauled the bales to the barn. A hay elevator whisked the bales up into the upper level where the two men stacked them for the coming winter. While the baling was going on, Joanne went back to mowing or raking. Dave, Jim, and Deborah spelled the workers and attended to other ranch chores as needed.

It took almost a week to fill the huge hay barn. After that, they stacked mountains of fresh hay in the center of two of the upper fields. The stacks were covered with huge tarpaulins and portable fence panels were put in place to keep the cattle out of the feed. It was a period of long hard days with everyone always in a hurry. It seemed like unwelcomed storm clouds threatened them almost every day, but they were lucky; as yet it hadn't rained. When a field had been cleared, the refreshing water was reapplied; and the growing cycle begun anew. This second growth would be the basis of their feed supply for the fall and early winter months. It wouldn't be long now before the large herd would be brought in from the hills, returning to the home place.

* * *

The clinic was coming along slowly. Deborah was advertising already and had a second phone line installed in the house. Dave watched the progress of the building as he went back and forth to town. He stopped one Saturday when he spotted Deborah's car and her new veterinary truck parked by the building. He had heard about the truck, but had not seen it before.

"Hi, Dave," she greeted.

"Looks like it's about ready to move into, Spider."

"Next week...Come, I'll show you around."

Deborah led him through the small office and waiting room and then to the kennel area and the surgical suite. The latter reminded him of similar rooms he had been frequenting in the past months.

All the shelves and storage areas looked to be well stocked. Out behind the building were several corrals and box stalls, all built under strong roofs to ward off sun and rain. Next to the corral stood a large tandem-axle horse trailer that could be used to transport up to four large animals at a time.

"Let me show you my new truck," Deborah proudly invited. "Picked it up yesterday in Missoula."

The big GMC four-wheel-drive pickup had a custom-designed bed. It was completely waterproof and had many compartments on either side that contained all the vet equipment, medicines, and supplies that she would need working in the field. At each corner on top of the cab were four floodlights, two facing forward and two to the rear. These could be swiveled to light any given area. The truck was also equipped with a powerful winch on the front bumper, a heavy-duty trailer hitch on the back, and a two-way radio. Another radio had been installed in the kitchen at the house and one in the small office complex at the clinic. Deborah was ready to roll.

"Our open house is Saturday," she stated. "My two girls will be here starting then. They both live in Hamilton."

"They have any experience in vet clinics?" Dave asked.

"One is a qualified vet assistant. The other's just a secretary. I guess they'll do all right. Time will tell. I'm going to take my truck home tonight and start driving it back and forth. I'll bring Jim down to get the Bronco later. You ready to go home?"

"I'll race you," Dave joked.

"No you won't."

They arrived at the house minutes later, and Deborah began fixing their supper. Jim was up in one of the fields changing the sprinklers with Ed, and Peggy was in her bedroom playing with Tiny.

"Don't fix anything for me, Spider," Dave said. "I'm going out on the town tonight."

"Big date?" the woman asked.

"She's not so big," he commented. "I'd say she was actually quite slim."

"Oh, Dave." Deborah laughed. "You know what I meant."

"Yeah, I know. Only teasing. Just eating at the restaurant and then maybe going dancing for a while. Time will tell."

Dave went into the living room and settled down for a few minutes on the couch. Peggy came in with her little beagle on a short leash. She sat down beside Dave.

"Gramps? Why do you call my mom a spider sometimes?"

"Not 'a spider,' just Spider," the man corrected. "Her daddy called her that when she was smaller than you are. When I came to work here, she wanted me to call her Spider. To make a long story short, I did."

"Oh," the child replied, seeming to be completely satisfied with the explanation.

Dave washed up and shaved and a short time later headed for town. The family sat down to their final meal of the day. They were just settling into their evening routine when Dave drove back into the yard. It was nearly dark by now. Deborah had just picked several apples from one of their trees when he arrived. She carried the fruit in her arms as she returned to the house.

"What happened, Dave?" she called.

"Betty's feeling a little under the weather tonight. Next week maybe…I'll see you in the morning." Dave waved, turned at once, and headed for the bunkhouse.

"Night, Dave," Deborah called. She shrugged her shoulders and, with a small armful of apples, headed back to the house intent on making an apple pie for tomorrow's dessert.

On Saturday morning, everything seemed to shift into high gear all at once. Dave, Jim, and the four ranch hands headed into the hills to haze their livestock back to the home place.

Deborah was up to her armpits with her open house at the new clinic, and Peggy accompanied her mother to the clinic for the day. They were all quite busy all morning, but then everything at the clinic slowed down for the lunch hour. Deborah hung a small sign on the front door, "Be back at 1:00." She and Peggy walked the two blocks to town. At Dave's favorite restaurant, she stopped for a moment's relaxation and a quick bite to eat.

"Hi, Deborah," Betty Johnson greeted. "What'll it be today? Hi, Peggy."

"Just a bowl of your clam chowder, Betty…And coffee."

"A cheeseburger for me," the child replied.

"Feeling better today?" Deborah asked.

"Feeling better?" the woman replied seemingly puzzled.

"Dave said you were a little under the weather last night."

Betty looked puzzled for a moment. "I never saw Dave last night. He never showed up."

"Oh, I must have misunderstood him," Deborah answered with a concerned frown.

The service was fast and the food very satisfying, and in no time, they were back at the clinic meeting many people during the long afternoon. By quitting time, Deborah had treated two cats, and four dogs. She held one dog over for the night in preparation for a surgical procedure in the morning. She also had an appointment, for the following day, to pregnancy test a small group of beef cows.

Back at the ranch, she found sheer bedlam as seemingly thousands of cattle milled about in the upper fields. In reality, it was only part of their herd. It would take Dave and the others several more days to get them all back inside the fence line.

After supper, Deborah walked with Dave down to the corral where Jim had just finished rubbing down the mounts that they had used that day. It was hot, dry, and dusty. Deborah picked up a lariat from the corral rails, shook out a loop, and deftly roped Dave's big gelding as it trotted past. She flipped a half hitch over the horse's nose and snubbed him to a fence post. She began rubbing the animal down for the second time.

"I saw Betty Johnson today," she began.

"Oh?"

"She said you didn't show up last night. Anything wrong, Dave?"

"No, nothing. I just suddenly felt pooped. It's been a tough couple of weeks. I didn't want you to worry, so I said that Betty backed out."

"No problems?" Deborah asked again.

"No problems," Dave replied.

Three days later the herd was all back home. They separated the bulls from the bunch and pastured them on a piece of land at the old Edwards' place. All the young stock were cut out, sorted, and marked for either market or replacements. The livestock haulers made their runs for two full days hauling the market animals to the auction yards up in Hamilton. For several days, the bedlam of bawling cows was nerve racking, as they lamented the loss of their offspring.

The regular cattle sale went off without a hitch and, once again, the animals of the Double Bar M brought close to the top-

THE BEST LAID PLANS OF MICE AND MEN...

dollar of the day. That night they all celebrated. The following day it was Deborah's turn to work the cattle. She buckled down to the first of five long days of steady employment as she pregnancy tested each of their two hundred breeding cows. They were lucky this year. She found only four out of the whole bunch that were open, without calves.

"That was probably the cheapest pregnancy testing you've ever had, Dave," the woman announced at the supper table that night.

"What do you mean by that?" he asked.

"Well, hell, Dave. I can't charge for testing my own herd now, can I...Or can I?"

"I don't see why not. It was a solid week's work for you. It'll look good on the clinic's balance sheet. Up here, we'll take it all off as an operations expense just like always. It really don't matter who we pay. Just send me a bill."

It was getting colder almost every day now. The irrigation systems had been turned off for the season; and the ditch had been shut down to just a trickle, leaving only enough to supply the needed water for the livestock. Their garden had been harvested and Joanne and Deborah had spent two long weekends freezing and canning various fruits and vegetables. Jim was working almost full time at the ranch now as Bert Mason, with the coming of colder weather, had lost interest in fishing. Peggy was enjoying her first days at school and Deborah's clinic was adding every week to its growing list of clients. It snowed in early November, but then along came Indian summer.

Deborah did the family wash one Saturday morning, as was her habit. When Dave came in from the barn, she caught his arm and stopped him in the kitchen.

"This was in the pocket of your jeans," she said, holding out the small pill bottle toward him. "Oh, thanks, Spider," he said, palming the empty bottle and slipping it into his pants' pocket.

"I read the label, Dave. That's awfully powerful, terribly dangerous stuff, you're taking. Mind telling me what's going on?" The deep concern of the moment was very obvious in her voice.

"Come walk with me, Spider," Dave suggested.

Deborah pulled on her fleece-lined Levi jacket, and they stepped out into the crisp fall air. Dave turned toward the corrals, slipped into the enclosure, and in just seconds managed to catch one of the horses by its mane. He flipped the lead rope from a halter around the animal's neck. Taking a currycomb from a nail high on the wall of the barn, he began to groom the animal. Deborah caught its head and nose in her strong hands and held the animal still.

"Well, Dave?" she finally asked.

"It's a long story, Spider...No, actually it's quite a short story, I guess. I really only found out back in April." There was a long pause. "Had a lot of headaches for no damned reason at all. Aspirin didn't help, and then it started to bother my vision... The attacks came and went pretty quick...I finally broke down and went to the VA Hospital up in Missoula, and I came away a condemned man." There was a seemingly endless break in their conversation.

"Go on, Dave," the woman finally pleaded, her voice steady, level, and controlled.

He shrugged. "Hell, they gave me maybe a year at the outside. They wanted chemo, radiation, the whole shooting match. But I've seen too many people over the years spend their few remaining months in the clutches of the doctors. I simply said no! To start with, they were happy that it seemed to be very slow growing. It's located way down at the very base of my skull right around the brain stem. Completely inoperative. But about a month ago they found that its growth had accelerated greatly. In early June, they gave me at the most six months. And there you have it."

Neither of them spoke for several minutes. Deborah finally reached up and took the currycomb from Dave's hand, slipped the halter rope from around the mare's neck. She slapped the horse on the rump, chasing her back into the corral. For long moments, the two people stood facing each other, and then her eyes filled with tears and she began to cry.

"Don't cry, Spider," Dave pleaded, reaching toward her.

"Cry with me, Dave," she begged.

He did. They fell into each other's arms and for a long while poured out their open grief. At last, they parted. Dave drew his handkerchief from the hip pocket of his jeans and wiped his face. Deborah ignored her tear-stained cheeks.

"How can I help you, Dave?" she asked quietly, almost professionally.

"Keep my secret as long as you can. Especially from Peggy. I don't want her to know. I won't ask you to keep it from Jim. That's asking too much."

"It's just life goes on like always?"

"That's about it."

"God help you," Deborah muttered. "I certainly can't."

"At the end you'll be here with me. That's all I can hope for."

"I'll be here," the woman promised. "Want some apple pie?" she asked. Arm in arm they turned toward the house.

* * *

For the following two weeks, the weather worsened. It was colder almost every night, and a few snow flurries sprinkled the hills. The haying equipment was overhauled as needed and stowed for the year, hay fields were fertilized with special blends determined by agricultural service soil tests, and routine ranch maintenance was carried on daily. On the tenth of November it snowed quite hard. They awoke that morning to about six inches of the white powder everywhere. After breakfast, Jim and Dave mounted the big snowplow blade on the front of the pickup. They didn't plow the road, but did shove a little back in the circular drive that curved around in front of their buildings. The cattle were browsing through the snow, still managing to find the young grass shoots, but Dave decided to start with their winter supplement anyway. They took the big International tractor with a hay stacker attachment out to the field, scooped up several big bunches of hay from one of the stacks, and scattered it in a long swath through the upper field. On top of this, they sprinkled a few big nuggets of a nutrient-rich grain supplement that the cattle gulped down eagerly.

Deborah was off to work every morning at the clinic, and she took Peggy the extra mile to school before settling down to her never-routine day. The business was slow going, but every week seemed to bring her at least one new customer. It would take time, she knew. Peggy always took the school bus home at night. It dropped her by the mailbox, and the little girl began walking the four-mile gravel road to the house. Someone almost always managed to meet her and provide a ride home. If the weather was too bad, she often stopped at Joanne's and waited for her ride. One snowy evening, Joanne gave Peggy a ride home. She dropped her off by the house and headed back home.

"Go get your old coat on, Peggy, and put on your ski pants too. Dress warm," Dave ordered.

While the child changed into her warm winter clothes Dave saddled his big gelding. From the equipment shed he produced an old toboggan that Peggy's mother had used many years ago.

"Get on," the man ordered and the child jumped aboard. Her little beagle leaped into her lap, and the girl wrapped one arm around the tiny dog, holding him close. Dave tied the end of his lariat to the toboggan's towrope and swung into the saddle. He took off at a walk as Peggy squealed happily. The little beagle wanted no part of this and immediately bailed out. Dave leaned from the saddle, opened a gate into the empty field below the house, and pulled the sled into the clear. "Ready?" he called back.

"Ready," Peggy shouted.

Dave picked his mount up into a fast trot and guided him through several large figure eights in the snowy field. This escalated a few minutes later into a fast lope with Peggy laughing excitedly every inch of the way. Her little dog ran and leaped through the snow behind her barking furiously, but he would not ride.

Flakes of fresh snow began to fall slowly from the solid slate-gray skies. The lights were on in the house, and Dave saw Ed Petron leave for the day heading home. A few minutes later Deborah climbed the hill and backed her vet truck into the open equipment shed next to the bunkhouse. Her day had been completed. As she walked toward the house, Dave headed for the gate. The woman stopped to watch, and she waited to greet her family as they pulled into the yard.

The front of the child's body was completely covered by snow. The hooves of Dave's horse had sent a constant deluge of flakes to engulf her. Her face was cherry pink, beaming with happiness. Dave swung down into the snowy yard, and the child hugged him eagerly.

"Thank you, Gramps," she cried. "Thank you so much."

"You go get dried off and warm," Deborah ordered.

"I am warm," Peggy replied.

"Go get warmer then. Shake off all that snow before you go inside. I'll make you some hot chocolate in a minute. Better rub that horse down good, Dave. You've worked him pretty hard," Deborah warned. As if understanding her words the horse snorted aloud sending a streamer of vapor into the frigid air.

"Yes, Ma'am," Dave replied and waved a quick salute as he turned and led the horse toward the corral.

He turned on the corral floodlight, cooled the animal down under the shelter of the loafing shed, rubbed him down well, and gave him a small grain ration. It was completely dark when he snapped off the light and headed toward the welcoming glow of the house. It was snowing harder now, and he knew there would be plenty to plow in the morning.

They ate supper and were all sitting about the living room when Deborah's business phone rang. She answered and talked for several minutes with the distant party, jotting down notes on a desk pad as she talked. At last, she hung up.

"Got to go," Deborah announced. "You know where the Timarco place is on the East Fork Road?"

"Afraid not. Brian Timarco?" Dave asked.

"Yes."

"I've met him, but don't know where his place is exactly."

"He's given me directions. I'll find it all right. He's got a mare foaling, and it doesn't look right to him."

"Want me to go with you?" Jim asked.

"No," was the emphatic reply. "I'll have my radio on if you need to get hold of me."

Deborah pulled on a pair of coveralls over her regular jeans and shirt and slipped into her winter coat. She kissed everyone good-bye, one by one, and hastily left the house. The lights of her truck vanished down the road a minute later.

The evening went well, Peggy headed for bed, and a few minutes later Dave finally called it quits. The skies had dropped at least two inches of snow since supper time.

He slipped into the bunkhouse and closed the door against the chill. Inside it was toasty warm. The electric heater always did an admirable job. Dave lay back on his bed and began flipping through a recent edition of a Stockman's publication. He tossed it over onto the chair beside the bed a few minutes later, pulled his bottle of pills from the pocket of his jeans, and downed two of the caplets. He closed his eyes against the light and tried to rest.

Dave didn't hear Deborah when she returned home at close to two in the morning. After a quick shower, she went directly to bed. She was up and about before the rest of her brood. The kitchen smelled of cinnamon and other spices when Jim and his daughter arrived. They were starting to eat when Deborah looked at Peggy and said, "Peggy, go yell at Dave. Tell him it's time to eat."

"OK," the child replied. She jumped from her seat, pulled on her winter coat and charged out the door. She was gone for several minutes and then returned. "I can't wake Gramps up," the child said, a puzzled look spreading across her face.

Deborah froze for a second and then burst from her chair so fast that the chair crashed backward onto the floor. The woman ran from the house not even stopping to grab her coat or hat. In the bunkhouse, the light was still on, and Dave lay fully clothed on his bed propped up slightly by his pillow.

"Dave?" Deborah called and then shouted, "Dave!" There was no response as she shook his shoulder. She grabbed at his neck trying to find a pulse. She ran to her truck and from the inside rearview mirror retrieved her stethoscope and returned to kneel at Dave's side. She was listening intently when Jim appeared.

"What is it?" the man asked.

"Jim, he's gone," Deborah whispered as tears poured down her cheeks. She settled back on her heels, pulled the earpieces of her stethoscope from her ears, and just let the instrument hang about her neck.

It was utterly silent in the room for a moment and then Jim blurted out, "Hey, I just saw him breathe."

Deborah nodded quietly. "Yes, I know, but it's about over."

"I'll call 9-1-1," Jim stated and turned toward the door.

"No, Jim! Let it go. He wanted to go this way. Will you go get Peggy ready for school? Just leave us alone."

Jim gripped his wife's shoulder and squeezed it in a sympathetic manner. He turned toward the door to leave.

"Don't call anyone, Jim…Please."

THE BEST LAID PLANS OF MICE AND MEN...

The man nodded and without comment left the room.

Deborah suddenly jumped to her feet and opened the door. She called after her husband. "Don't tell Peggy just yet; let me do it."

She returned to Dave's side and sat quietly on the edge of the bed. She pulled the neatly folded bedspread up over his body and listened again to the faint, struggling pulses of his heart. His skin was cold and moist with sweat, his breathing rare and labored. Minutes passed and she listened again. Now there was nothing that she could detect. She tried for probably five minutes to find some sign of life, but there was nothing. She finally collapsed across Dave's body and wept openly as the reality sank in.

Deborah rose reluctantly several minutes later and opened the door. She stood there in the open doorway with the falling snow peppering her upturned face. She wanted to give out a piercing scream of agony, but somehow remained silent. Then she began to sob almost silently.

"What is it, Mom?" a voice whispered. "What's happened?"

Deborah jumped and looked down at the shocked face of her daughter. The child stood in the falling snow with no coat or hat. She had sensed that something was wrong and bolted from the house.

"What's wrong, Mama?" the little girl asked again and craned her neck to look past her mother into Dave's room.

Deborah pulled her child into the shelter of the bunkhouse and quietly closed the door. She pulled her stethoscope from around her neck and slipped the ear tips into her daughter's ears. She then held the instrument to Dave's chest for a long moment.

After a while, Peggy looked up at her mother and said, "I don't hear anything."

"I know, honey. Your grandpa's gone. He's died."

"But...?"

"It's over, honey. He loved your Grandma Peg very much, and now he's gone to be with her."

"But why, Mama?"

Deborah answered with difficulty struggling to speak through her own grief. "I really don't know, Peggy. Gramps has been sick for a long time, and there wasn't anything that anyone could do for him. He didn't want to go to the hospital. He wanted to stay here with you and me just as long as he could. I've got a long letter that he wrote to you. He asked me to give it to you after he was gone. I'll get it for you when you want to read it."

"Can I have it now?" Peggy asked.

"Let's go to the house," Deborah replied. "I'll get it for you, and help you read it." She switched off the light and, hand in hand, they walked through the falling snow toward the brightly lighted house.

-0-

Made in the USA
Charleston, SC
09 April 2011